The Arizona Panhandle

Richard Clarke

Walker and Company
New York

Also by Richard Clarke

The Arrowhead Cattle Company
The Peralta Country
The Homesteaders
The Copperdust Hills

First published in the United States of America in 1989
by Walker Publishing Company, Inc.

Published simultaneously in Canada by Thomas Allen & Son
Canada, Limited, Markham, Ontario

Library of Congress Cataloging-in-Publication Data

Clarke, Richard, 1916–
The Arizona panhandle / Richard Clarke.
p.   cm.
ISBN 0-8027-4098-7
I. Title.
PS3566.A34A87   1989
813'.54—dc20   89-9003
CIP

Printed in the United States of America

10 8 6 4 2 1 3 5 7 9

CHAPTER 1

The South Desert

IT was Mormon country and there were only two ways to get there unless a rider came east by way of the Grand Canyon, or from the west where water was as scarce as hen's teeth.

To get down there from the north a man had to ride through the St. George settlement of Utah. From the south he had to cross the huge Navajo Reservation, and depending on the time of year, he could come up from the south without being detected, providing he made the excursion before spring, when the tribesmen scattered to ancestral rancherias held individually by different clans. If he waited until the clans were abroad with their sheep, his passage would be noted, even if he rode by moonlight.

Ashe Colby knew practically nothing about The People or their reservation, but he chose to cross the Navajo Reservation because he knew there had to be water there, and being desert-born and -bred, he was mindful that the South Desert country would be hot and dry now that springtime had yielded to summer.

If a saddlehorseman tried to cross the desert after the blooms turned to flowers and shriveled, he would find no relief from the heat, even if he holed up during the day and rode by night. This was a lesson learned by those who had watched hundreds of wayfarers start out too late and never return. Such wisdom was the best kind: tales of unbelievable suffering and death made a lasting impression.

At thirty-five Ashe Colby had heard the stories. Even if he hadn't, he knew perfectly well what any horseman would

1

face who tried to reach the Wolf Hole country of the Arizona Strip from the south, even in early springtime.

But it was not unusual for absolute necessity to compel human beings to act unwisely out of desperation. As Colby sat atop a fat, round hill that was covered with tiny wildflowers, looking into the northward distance where everything between heaven and earth was hostile, he told his mule-nosed bay horse that if the Good Lord would hold off just a little while before making his judgment, Colby and the bay horse might make it.

He swung around in the saddle, placed one palm on the bay horse's rump, and scanned empty country for as far as he could see.

There was no dust hanging in the air, no tiny dark specks moving back there, no sunlight reflecting off cheekpieces, spurs, or metal butt-plates.

He faced forward again, tugged at each glove, and kneed the mule-nosed horse down off the hilltop, then headed straight northward.

The hour before dawn and the hour after dawn were almost a spiritual experience on the springtime desert. The air was refreshingly cool. It was also as clear as glass and softly fragrant with the scent of tiny, shy flowers. The silence was a depthless continuum from the beginning of time. Small cactus wrens hurried between sahuaros, while trap-door spiders and hairy tarantulas as broad as the back of a man's hand scuttled for food before holing up against the heat. Some less admirable creatures such as the sluggish Gila monster and desert rattler, neither of which could stand excessive heat, prowled for the same reason—to get a meal before the heat drove them to cover.

Colby's bay horse was short-backed, muscled-up, deep-chested, and sensible. He was a horseman's animal; petting made him uncomfortable, yet when he was hobbled to forage he never went too far away to be able to see his master.

The relationship was a good one. It was founded, on the

horse's part, upon an unquestioning willingness to do as the man asked. On Colby's part, he was solicitous of the animal's welfare and protective and respectful toward the horse. He would have treated his horse that way even if the mule-nosed bay hadn't been such a good partner, because Ashe Colby was a horseman. Not a rider—anyone could become a rider and most people did. All that was required to become a rider was for a person to spread his legs and pull a horse under him. Genuine horsemanship was one-third in the saddle and two-thirds on the ground.

Colby and the bay horse made good time and steady progress for three days. Both knew enough of the land's secrets to determine where water might be, but early spring-time offered many pools that, within six weeks when full summer arrived, would be as dead as a tortoise shell.

For a week, man and horse moved through a seemingly endless array of wind-sculpted sandstone spires and across hundreds of barren miles of tan-tawny, sterile soil. The very limited forage grew only on the east side of grotesque stone plinths, or close to the base of sahuaros and lacy paloverde trees, or in the midst of catclaw, creosote bush, and other varieties of understory that most animals avoided because of thorns. Neither the horse nor his rider looked any the worse for their hardships, which was basically because neither of them had embarked upon their odyssey without already being trimmed down to bone, nerve, and muscle.

They had seen one other two-legged creature. A bronco astride an ancient flea-bit gray horse, moccasined feet dangling down the sides of a beast whose every rib showed. The old Indian was blanketed to the poll. He was not a village Indian; he did not wear a hat. From the distance separating him from Colby, the Navajo looked like a conical stick-man riding a ghost-horse. He was traveling in a southeasterly direction, leaving barefoot horse tracks in a waste where the next largest quadruped sign had been made by one of those big, slab-sided desert rabbits.

The bronco had evidently been riding since before dawn, perhaps all night. He was wrapped inside his blanket even after sunrise when the chill was swiftly diminishing.

Colby turned back a short distance westerly to the place where he'd spent the night, dismounted at the sump-spring, loosened the cincha, draped his bridle from the horn, and this time, although it was not a wise thing to do in a land where no one survived on foot very long, neglected to hobble the bay horse as he went up a low hill to look upcountry. The old bronco could have been riding for a week, but however long he'd been astride, he had come from somewhere; there were other people out there. Somewhere.

But even though it was the hour just after dawn and the best time of day for studying desert distances, Colby could see nothing. No mud hogans, no tin roofs, no windmills, corrals, not even any dust from goat and sheep pens. Nothing.

He mounted his bay and turned directly northward, only veering a little easterly when he sought the old Indian's tracks.

There were no tracks. Perhaps another few miles east there were, but Ashe did not waste any more effort on anything as unimportant as satisfying his curiosity. He faced northward again.

In an empty vastness such as this there was little to occupy a man's thoughts except memories, and in Ashe Colby's case there was little he cared to recall, so instead he thought about the old bronco on his bone-rack horse.

For two eventual reasons he abandoned his speculations. One reason was that he did not know enough about The People to make a sound judgment. The other reason appeared so unexpectedly that the bay horse grunted and shied so violently sideways that Colby lost a stirrup.

A little vixen fox had darted from the shadows on the west side of one of those abruptly rising, grotesque stone plinths to lunge with bared fangs at what she perceived not only as an intruder, but also as a direct threat to her three tiny, ginger-colored pups in their cool underground den.

Colby stopped, turned the horse to face the yapping, whining, flat-eared, menacing small animal, and noticed that one of her reasons for aggravation was the hole at the base of the spire she was protecting; the other reason was a badly inflamed and swollen forepaw.

He studied the emaciated body, the lusterless fur, the pain-filled, wild eyes, and by the time the vixen's snarls were diminishing, he detected little whining sounds from the dark hole at the base of the spire. Three gaunt, unkempt, and clearly starving pups were peering from the den-hole.

Colby took down his lariat. Roping a fox, which was by nature a very nervous animal and never still for more than a moment, required a very uncommon skill.

Colby moved the horse a fraction in order to force the vixen to think of escape in the opposite direction, then swung twice and made his cast in that direction, leading the tiny animal about her own length.

When she came to the end of the rope, felt it closing around her throat, she sprang into the air, somersaulted, snarled, bit, pawed, and lunged in wild terror.

Colby dismounted and waited until the vixen was on her belly—ears pinned flat, eyes malevolent with terror, fangs bared in a genuine threat—then took two steps forward. The vixen had eighteen inches of slack and used it in a whirling dash that sent her head over heels when Colby picked up the slack. He had to repeat this three times before he got her choked down.

She fainted.

He went forward and before loosening the rope enough for her to breathe, he very carefully tied her jaws closed with his bandana.

Even when he loosened the rope enough for the vixen's bursting lungs to fill with oxygen, he did not remove the rope. He dragged her over into horse-shade, where the mule-nosed bay watched everything with wary interest as Colby secured three of the vixen's legs, left the injured foot free. When the vixen regained consciousness it was to the stinging pain of a knifeblade lancing her foot. She fought like a little tiger without the man making any effort to restrain her more than he had to.

As pus gushed from the infected foot, the vixen alternately growled and whimpered in her throat, beat her head on the ground, and strained fruitlessly against her bonds. Colby paid very little attention as he rinsed the wound from his canteen, dug out the cause of the infection—a pus-softened and whitened cactus thorn—and rinsed the wound a second time. He worked almost effortlessly, without expression, without soothing words, until he'd done all that could be done. Then he released the vixen's jaws, pocketed the bandana, and brought her three pieces of pepper-cured jerky from his saddlebags.

The vixen's bloodshot eyes were glazed. She would not take the meat, so Colby went over to the mouth of the den where tiny puffballs were instinctively hovering just out of reach. He placed the cured meat inside the hole and sat back waiting.

A squawling scramble ensued as hunger overrode fear and the fox pups rushed to tear at the jerky.

Colby smiled, returned to the vixen, tipped a sparing amount of water down her open mouth, which she had to swallow to avoid strangling, then got everything ready before releasing the vixen. He stood beside his horse as she went racing wildly, erratically away. The vixen would survive. She would lick her wound until it healed.

The horse lost interest. The bay was standing like a statue, head up, ears pointed northeastward, his full attention on something he could either see or smell but which Colby never did locate as he swung astride and turned due north with half an hour left before the heat would begin its day-long stalk.

He looked back, but even the spire itself was now just another receding part of the past. He straightened around and did what all solitary riders did, he spoke to his horse, whose reaction to the noise coming from the two-legged rider on its back was to show as little interest as it had over the last three years since they'd formed their partnership. The bay horse ignored him.

"Horse, you ever get the feeling that whether you do good or bad, it don't make any difference to any damned creature except two-legged ones?"

The horse walked along, watching up ahead. He no longer even cocked back his ears when his rider made those noises.

CHAPTER 2

Wolf Hole

IN early springtime it was possible to continue on the trail well into the afternoon, but only three weeks later it would not be; the heat would make it impractical.

From the moment Colby and the mule-nosed horse struck camp before sunrise and adhered to their northward course, there was just one sign they watched for throughout the day: water.

As Colby told the bay horse, it might have helped if either of them had ever been in this country before. There had to be water somewhere. The Indians knew where it was; Colby did not know, so while the bay horse walked along on a loose rein using his nose to detect vestiges of dampness in the air, the man on his back watched for indications of old Navajo habitations. He had found several—and water—since embarking across this immense wasteland of eternal silence.

In another week or two, owners of those ancestral camps would come straggling along, their herds of sheep and goats out ahead.

Once, he bedded down beside one of those mud-wattle hogans with the smoke-hole in the roof still covered against winter weather and where the log-framed single doorway facing east, always east, appeared as a dark, square opening. There was a stoned-up circular spring about five yards from the hogan.

The hogan looked like an inverted beehive and the water in the stoned-up spring looked like the sky: turquoise blue.

What predominated here, too, was silence. Complete, total silence.

It was at this place he saw his second human being. Colby had hobbled the bay horse near some scraggly new growth, was foraging for fagots to make his beans-and-coffee fire when he happened to look out where the horse should have been cropping grass. Instead, the bay was standing like a carving, head high, ears forward, eyes fixed upon a westerly, long-spending, curving rib of land.

There was a horseman sitting atop the low ridge facing Colby's uninhabited rancheria. He was too distant for details to be discernible, but as Colby straightened up with an armload of fagots, he was sure it had to be an Indian.

The rider sat out there like a statue, motionless, watching, silent. When dusk shadowed the world with its faint sootiness, the rider was no longer visible.

Colby made his supper, afterward rolled and lit a smoke, and speculated that the Indian probably owned this hogan-area. Or if he didn't, he knew who did, and probably also knew that Colby was not the owner. He certainly knew Colby was not an Indian: he'd sat out there long enough watching everything Colby did to be sure of that.

The bay horse was back hopping in search of forage. Colby went out there to squat and watch him for a while, then returned to the hogan, spread his groundsheet, unrolled his blanket, shed his boots with the spurs intact, used his sweat-smelly saddle blanket as a pillow, and rolled up onto his side, doing everything very deliberately to provide a watcher with a convincing enactment.

Fifteen minutes later, utilizing full darkness, he shoved the saddle blanket under the bedding, left his hat close by along with his spurred boots, took his handgun, and padded silently around behind the hogan to wait.

It was a very long and unproductive wait. By the approach of dawn, the hour had arrived to leave. He had heard and seen nothing, and evidently neither had the mule-nosed horse, which Colby had relied upon to help him in his vigil. Nothing had disturbed the bay during the night.

After a meager breakfast he rigged out, stepped astride, and with one gloved palm resting lightly on the butt of his booted saddlegun, urged the bay horse due north again.

Neither man nor horse detected anything as they rode— no movement, no motionless manshapes. For the first time, Ashe Colby was uneasy. He blamed it on both the silence and the land's emptiness, which stretched as far as his eye could see. He'd undertaken this trip particularly by this route because he had to arrive in the Wolf Hole country unde-tected. Now, although he was certain the first bronco had not seen him, he knew for a fact the second one had.

What he had to know was which way this observer had gone after he'd departed, but as had happened before, when he scouted up the curving rib of land he found no tracks.

That puzzled him, but what really caused worry was that if the observer had ridden northward, he could possibly be heading for a place where there were other people. He would probably tell them what he'd seen: a solitary horseman who was not a Navajo, coming upcountry from someone's ances-tral rancheria.

If he told this only to other Indians, then Colby's situation would not be as bad as if the observer told his story to a settlement of non-broncos.

Colby knew one particular thing about the country he was heading for; it was inhabited by insular, suspicious people. They were scattered over many miles of an inhospitable countryside. They had a reputation for fierce independence, and with no authorized lawman nearer than St. George, ninety miles north of their isolated community at Wolf Hole, administration of the law was subject to personal, individual caprice.

He had to hope that the spying Indian did not ride that far north.

For three more days he kept to his established heading

without seeing another human being. Once, he saw a band of wild horses raising dust as they raced away from whatever had stampeded them. He watched intently for the cause of their panic, did not find it, and rolled a smoke as he allowed this event to leave his mind.

Ashe Colby knew wild horses. He'd trapped them since boyhood, not always with much success but with just enough to keep him at it for several years. And if there was one thing he'd learned about *mesteños,* it was that when they panicked the reason could be anything from an abrupt flight of birds rising underfoot to the appearance on their flank of a band of mangy coyotes, from a rock cracking under extreme summer heat to the faintest scent borne on errant breezes of human beings miles away.

The land was beginning to change, very subtly but noticeably. Bunch grass began to appear, scraggly, unhealthy looking at first, then stronger, darker, and in closer clumps. Also, there were gray rocks, initially no larger than a man's head but eventually much larger—in places taller than a mounted man—and in tumbled fields of loose array.

One day he saw three trees growing close to one another at the base of a nearly precipitous stone bluff. Atop the bluff, only partially visible, were other trees.

Finally he was putting the empty land behind him, but this new country, while certainly more likely to support livestock, was just as utterly silent and menacing in its own way as the land he'd just passed through.

He made a camp beside a little trickle of warm water that flowed southward. Nothing but ground-hugging underbrush grew along the creekbanks.

Away from the creek, there were dusty-looking varieties of taller brush, occasionally in thickets but mostly individual plants growing several feet high.

By Colby's reckoning, he had arrived in the vicinity of the place he wanted to find. It was livestock country, but although he found dried cow chips, he did not find any fresh ones. He assumed the reason for this was that he was at the southernmost tip of the Wolf Hole country, where feed was less abundant than it was farther north. Stockmen would keep their animals upcountry.

The next day he followed the little warm-water creek. Somewhere, in this nearly waterless country, there would be either a ranch or a village near the creek.

What he found was an old wild-horse trap made of fagots. It hadn't been used recently, most likely because—with flowing water in the creeks and buffalo grass in its seasonal prime—trapping mustangs would be a lot more difficult now than later, after other creeks ran dry and the grass cured, when the horses could be enticed into the trap, providing its water was still flowing.

Experienced enough at reconnoitering new country to seek a high place, Colby rode to the top of a granite plateau. Up there amid a few trees and an expanse of stirrup-high grass, he could see for miles. He saw a village about four miles northwesterly. There was no other visible settlement. Because the air was as clear as glass he could see a great distance, but the only buildings he saw, aside from the settlement, were a few set miles apart and very far from the settlement.

If that bronco had not come up this far, and there were reasons why he wouldn't, Colby would have plenty of time to scout the land and settle in.

He took out a tiny metal compass, held it on his palm until he'd located true northeast, checked the degrees to be sure, then whittled a clear area around one small upturning juniper limb and hung his steel mirror from it. With the limbs cut away, the juniper would expose the mirror to the sun's rays most of the day. Unless of course the sky clouded up. He doubted that would happen. He hadn't seen a decent-sized cloud since he'd entered the reservation.

Leaving the plateau, he meandered up the creek for a couple of miles before finding a place with a tree for shade where he set up his camp, this time with signs of more or less permanency.

He loafed for one full day, washed his clothing in the creek, bathed, lay in speckled shade watching the bay horse crop grass heads, and methodically reviewed a number of things in his mind.

The following day was different. He made a miles-wide scout, searched for and found an isolated ranch, and sat back a mile in a field of big rocks watching the buildings. He knew there were people down there because he saw a lazy spindrift of smoke rising from the kitchen stovepipe, but he did not see a single human being.

When he wearied of the vigil and was turning back to his hobbled horse, a door slammed. The sound carried for an inordinate distance in this desolate place.

Someone—it looked to be a lithe young boy—came from the main house and headed for the old barn. It was covered by a bleached and heat-curled slab roof. The boy was carrying something and his head was partially hidden by the brim of a large old hat.

Colby had seen no horses in the corrals out behind the barn. Ten minutes later the boy emerged from the barn into the yard out front, turned a saddled animal twice, and swung across leather.

It was not at all unusual for stockmen to keep a horse or two in the barn. But most of the horses were usually kept in corrals.

Colby returned to the bay horse, snugged up, set the bridle, hung the hobbles, and stepped up, not to trail the youth but to utilize as much concealment as he could while he kept the youth in sight.

When he was satisfied the lad was heading for Wolf Hole with its one long, barracks-like building and several smaller structures, he eyed the position of the sun and decided that if he waited to trail the youth on his way back to the ranch, it would be too dark to do so effectively. He faded back farther, then turned southward in the direction of his camp.

He was not as interested in the lad as he was the ranch, which looked run-down, old, and uncared-for.

The following morning he rode back up there. This time the stove-smoke was rising straight up; someone was cooking at the main house. There were three saddled animals dozing at a tie-rack down in front of the barn.

There was no sign of the boy or any horses other than those at the tie-rack. For that matter there was no sign of this being a working cattle ranch. As he sat in relaxed conceal-ment wondering if he could be lucky enough, after only a few days in the Wolf Hole country, to have found what he'd ridden his tailbone raw to find, three men appeared on the dilapidated porch of the main house. All Colby could make out was that they were large, burly individuals wearing faded clothing. They stood a moment before starting toward the saddled animals in front of the barn.

He could also see that they were armed, not only with beltguns but with booted carbines under the *rosadero* of each saddle.

When they left the yard at a dead walk, they did not do as he expected—head toward the settlement. Instead, they rode loosely northeastward. Being a saddlehorseman himself, Col-by's guess was that whichever way they would eventually go, at this early stage of their travels they were only indifferently heading that way; it could be north or it could be east.

To his knowledge, which had been gained atop that plateau where he'd left the steel mirror, there were no nearby ranches or settlements in either direction.

He made no attempt to follow the horsemen. For an additional hour or so he watched the ranch. The only move-ment down there occurred when a rawboned, tall, gaunt woman came forth to fling dishwater into a bed of scraggly geraniums. She paused a moment to regard the pathetic flowers, which were the only indication Colby could see that even hinted someone in that old house had another side to his or her soul than the kind of bare-bones existence people in this kind of place struggled to maintain.

Colby returned to his camp. He had not seen the lithe youth from yesterday. He wondered whether the kid had saddled up a horse and ridden toward Wolf Hole before Colby arrived this morning.

What Colby did know was that instead of riding toward the settlement this time, the lad had made a meandering ride in a sashaying way, crossing from east to west until, up near those fortress-rocks where Colby had watched, the youth stopped stone-still and sat a long while looking at fresh, shod-horse sign.

If Colby had seen this he would have expected the youth to streak it for the ranch. The lad did just the opposite. After dismounting, leading his horse by the reins while he back-tracked the shod-horse sign, the youth finally did swing back over leather, but only to make better progress as he under-took a tracking odyssey that, fortunately, had to end when daylight failed. Then, finally, the youth turned back toward home.

CHAPTER 3

Breakfast

THE following day Colby drank black coffee, ate beans mixed with rabbit meat, and smoked a leisurely cigarette. Then he rode up toward the plateau where he'd left his steel mirror in the juniper tree.

By the time he arrived, enough sunlight was reflecting off the mirror to satisfy him that it was still in place, so he turned back—and had his attention snagged by distant movement. He stood still, watching a distant rider passing in and out of shadowy, tall stands of underbrush.

Whoever he was, he was taking his time. He was also doing something else; he was riding down Ashe Colby's shod-horse sign from the direction of that old ranch. (Only rarely did the people in this country shoe their horses. If Colby had known that, he could have pulled the bay horse's shoes. But it was too late now.)

Colby waited until the tracker was within a mile of his camp, riding directly toward it, then led the bay horse into cover. His intention was to allow the tracker to get down to the camp, then Colby would come up behind him.

What happened to this plan, like most plans clever men make, was that it did not end as it was supposed to. Colby was leaving the bay horse, on his way back to the rim where he could keep track of the oncoming rider, when the world exploded inside his head, the sun winked out, and blackness came, accompanied by one very brief but excruciating moment of pain.

The world continued to be dark. When he came to, Colby

17

had no idea how much time had passed. His head felt like he was recovering from a week-long drunk. He lay in blackness with water streaming from both eyes, with his stomach alternately knotting and unknotting as he raised a faltering hand to feel his head.

The hair was matted with semi-dry blood. He had a lump nearly as large as a goose egg. He also had no shell-belt or gun; his hat was lying close by, with a rat half the size of a cat gnawing where stains of salt-sweat marked the juncture between the brim and the crown. He waved a shaking hand to make the rat flee.

At first he was not aware of gruff voices, although he wrinkled his nose at the fragrance of cooking. Instead of arousing hunger, the cooking smell made him want to vomit.

It was night. He was lying on some old, brown army blankets in a small room with a stone floor. When he groped to his right, his hand encountered a jug of water. He would have preferred whiskey. Each time he moved, the sickening sensation returned, but he cupped water in one hand and trickled it over the big lump. It had no effect on his headache, but it did wash some of the blood from his head and carry it down the front of his clothing.

He drank a little of the water, pushed the jug aside, and sat up. Immediately, a light-headed sensation made him push against the floor with both hands. This feeling was followed by intense pain that seemed to fluctuate with his pulse beat.

Finally he heard the gruff voices, but evidently because the door to his prison was thick, he could not distinguish words.

The realization of what must have happened came very gradually. While he'd been spying on that rider who had been tracking him, someone else had come up on him from behind.

He had been ambushed as though he were a wet-behind-the-ears kid. He'd fallen for one of the oldest tricks in the world. Colby had been baited into concentrating on the visible rider while an accomplice caught him from behind.

He trickled water over his head until it seemed some of the pain was diminishing. Whether this was attributable to the water or to the fact that he'd been lying in this little room since morning, at least six hours after he'd been hit over the head, was arguable. But right at this moment all Ashe Colby was concerned about was the lessening of the headache.

Someone wearing spurs approached the heavy door. Colby eased back down as the door was cracked a few inches. He kept his eyes closed and his breathing ragged until the door was opened wider, allowing a lamp someone was holding high to brighten the room. A bullnecked man whose hair grew down both temples and across half his low, gorilla-like forehead stepped in with a six-gun in his fist. Behind him, an equally unshorn and unkempt-looking individual also entered. He was holding a coal-oil lamp in his right hand. He said, "You killed him, Joseph."

The bullnecked, big, burly man's reply was gruff. "All right. I killed him."

They came to stand over Colby. The one called Joseph took the lamp and held it down as he said, "He's breathing."

His companion leaned down. "He is, for a fact." Then, straightening up, he added, "But sure as hell you busted his skull. He'll die."

That didn't trouble Joseph either. "Then we'll bury him and add a good horse to what we already got."

"Joseph, what about the wanted dodger?"

Colby almost forgot the agony behind his eyes. That wanted poster with his likeness on it had been in his saddle-bags at his permanent camp. If that's all they found—good.

Joseph was scratching inside his shirt when he spoke again. "What about it? He's a stage an' bank robber."

The other man sounded almost sarcastic when he answered. "Three thousand dollars reward."

Joseph stopped scratching and leaned far down. "Hell, he's got blood all down the front of him."

"Three thousand dollars, Joseph."

"An' just how do we collect it, Sam'l?"

"Haul his carcass up to St. George, hand it over to the law, an' put in a claim."

Joseph put a testy glare upon his companion. "You never think, do you? The law'll ask questions. They might even ride down here to make an investigation."

Samuel seemed reluctant to abandon the idea of collecting a large reward. "Three thousand dollars . . ."

Joseph brushed his companion aside as he went back to the door. "Let him die in peace. Leave him be. We'll come back in the morning. By then he ought to be stiff as a ramrod."

As they were closing the door, barring it from the outside, Colby heard Samuel whine again about the reward, but this time he got no response from the burly man who went clanking back to some other part of the house.

Colby did not sit up again for a long time. He was in the hands of some completely indifferent men. He derived a little satisfaction from the fact that they had found that wanted dodger. That just might keep him alive. If they came back in the morning and he was feeling up to it, he'd tell them a story that, if they believed it—and care would have to be taken to make it sound believable—they might want to keep him alive.

He was lying there when sleep arrived. He had not expected to be able to sleep. When he awakened, while he was still sore all over and any kind of head movement brought a reminder that he'd been hit hard, his headache was gone as long as he did not move.

He knew it was daylight because people were stirring in the house. Also, he could hear chickens outside, noisily scratching close to the west side of the house. He thought his little prison probably had once been a storeroom, for perhaps edibles that required a cool, dark place. Stone floors were uncommon anywhere, except in storerooms.

He heard someone coming and pushed up into a sitting position with his back to the south wall. His clothing was still damp but the bleeding from his head wound had stopped. He suspected he must have looked every bit as bad as he felt, maybe even worse. For one thing he hadn't been able to shave; for another, he considered it to his advantage to appear very badly injured.

When the door opened, the same two men as before entered—the big, powerful man named Joseph and his thin, rawboned friend, Samuel. It was Samuel who was in front this time with the lamp. He stopped and gasped at the sight of their prisoner sitting on the floor across the room.

Joseph roughly pushed past his companion, then also stopped. After a long moment he said, "Well, well. Mister Colby, you don't look very good but at least you're alive. For how long, I don't know. Can you stand up?"

Colby made a feeble effort and sank back without saying a word.

Joseph walked over, got a fistful of soggy shirtfront, and hoisted Colby to his feet and held him there. "We got some breakfast for you," he said, showing big, worn-down white teeth in a mirthless smile.

Joseph supported Colby as they walked out of the little room, down a long corridor with a bare plank floor, and into a large kitchen. There the lanky woman Colby had seen dump water in a geranium bed was standing at the stove. She twisted half around to watch the three men enter the room.

Another man was already seated at an old table, forking in food as though he hadn't eaten in several days. He was older than the other men, probably a couple of years older than the woman with the pursed mouth and baleful gray eyes, but all he did was raise his eyes—he did not raise his head or pause from his breakfast.

Joseph shoved Colby down on a chair and growled for

Samuel to fetch some food, which Samuel did without any hesitation. It was the woman who spoke first as the men were stabbing steaks off a platter and noisily drinking black coffee. She said, "He looks like the picture on the dodger."

Joseph spared her a glance. "What was you expectin', Santa Claus?"

The woman turned her back on them while the older man, who was mopping his plate with a piece of coarse bread, smiled at Colby. "You didn't really come up here from down south, did you?"

Before Colby could answer, the older man spoke again. "Maybe you cut in from the east somewhere. I heard someone blew a bank safe over in Riverton, about a hunnert miles east. Would that have been you, Mister Colby?"

Colby sipped coffee without replying, until the older man, still grinning, arose to fish in a cupboard and returned to tip some whiskey into Colby's cup and wink as he sat down again. "Accordin' to your dodger, you been awful busy the last few years. Tell me somethin', Mister Colby; if what that dodger says is true, you ain't had enough time to spend all that loot, have you?"

Colby was beginning to feel human again. Before answering, he tipped a little more whiskey into his coffee and went back to eating. Then he eyed the old man and said, "It takes money to keep clear. Sometimes it takes a lot of money."

The old man had already got an idea fixed in his head and would not abandon it. "Yes, I expect it does. A man don't escape as often as the poster says you have without it costin' him a lot of money." He dropped a sly wink in Colby's direction. "I had a cousin once, years back, who had to pay five hunnert dollars as regular as clockwork every time he escaped. He told me every time he raided a town or stole mail sacks, he just naturally figured five hunnert from whatever he got was to pay for an escape. Is that about how you figure things, Mister Colby?"

Colby continued to eat as he nodded at the older man.

It was the burly Joseph who snarled at them both. "You two think this is some kind of damned game? I don't." He turned on Colby with a knife in one fist and a fork in the other fist. "We done some calculatin'. We come up with somethin' like six thousand dollars you got to have cached somewhere." He paused to watch Colby, who continued to eat without looking up. Then Joseph put down the fork, but still gripped the knife as he spoke again. "Mister, you better talk when folks're addressin' you."

Colby looked up, swallowed, and spoke. "An' if I tell you where the cache is, you turn me loose on my horse?"

Joseph's malevolent gaze did not waver. He had recognized the sarcasm. "You don't have no choice," he replied.

Colby answered while looking the big man in the eye. "Yes, I have. The minute I tell you where the cache is, I'm a dead man. Mister, if I don't tell you, I'm still a dead man. So if I go to hell, at least you fellers won't have none of my money in your pockets after I'm gone."

The burly man began coming up off his chair, still clutching the knife. His face was twisted in fury as the older man reached, gave him a sharp stab under the ribs, and said, "Sit down!" There was a world of menace in those two words.

Joseph sat down but did not take his eyes off Colby as the older man smiled again, pushed the bottle closer to Colby, and said, "You don't want to pay too much attention to Joseph. He's my firstborn. I expect me'n the missus spoiled him somethin' scandalous."

Samuel smiled at the old man and said, "Joseph'll get it out of him, Paw. Just leave 'em alone in that storeroom for a spell. Joseph'll have him begging to tell us where his cache is."

The old man continued. "Now then, Sam'l, you know the Christian way's the best. Your maw's been tellin' you boys that since you was buttons. . . . Mister Colby, it'd help a lot if you'd give this some real hard thought. You got to remember you're a wanted man with three thousand dollars on your

head. Now then, you think about this: We can take you up to
St. George, hand you over an' put in for the reward. Or we
can turn you loose after you've told us where the cache is.
Mister Colby, it's sort of like sittin' on a rock or a hard place,
ain't it? But you're not goin' nowhere until you make up your
mind. If I was in your boots, I'd cooperate."

Colby returned the man's unctuous, humorless smile and
replied, "Like I said, Mister . . . ?"

"Mister Rigdon. Sidney Rigdon."

"Glad to make your acquaintance, Mister Rigdon. Like I
was saying, I'm not goin' to ride away from here either way."

"Oh now, boy," exclaimed the old man, eyes round with
injury. "Of course you are. All we want is the money. You got
my word on the Gospel about that. You'll be free to ride
anywhere you want the moment we know where the money's
hid. Like I just said, you got my word on it." The old man's
sincerity overflowed. "Missus Rigdon, make up a poultice for
Mister Colby's bump, will you?"

The woman, whose back had been to the table since Colby
had entered the kitchen, did not face around now. Nor did
she act as though she'd heard her husband speak.

CHAPTER 4

The Family

THEY returned Colby to his prison, barred the door from the outside, and left him in darkness. That rat was after his hat the moment he put it aside, so he removed a boot and hurled it.

He might have connected; at least the rat squeaked several times.

As Colby was pulling the boot on, he heard an argument erupt in the far end of the house, near where he thought the kitchen was. It continued furiously for a couple of minutes, then ended.

An hour later, when he was wishing he had more of that whiskeyed coffee, old Sidney Rigdon unbarred the door, came in, and parked a lamp on a wall-stand. He stood smiling with his back against the door.

Colby was seated on the floor at the opposite side of the room, and as long as the old man had an old, long-barreled six-gun on his right side, the distance was too great. Even assuming the old man might not be as fast as he'd been thirty years earlier, the risk was not worth taking. Ashe Colby had seen men as old as this one who were very good with handguns.

Rigdon made no move to touch his weapon as he walked over and dropped something in Colby's lap. It was a pony of malt whiskey. As he stepped back, Rigdon said, "Now then, let's you'n me do some serious talking." He made a deprecating wave with one sinewy hand. "Don't pay too much attention to Joseph. He's big an' spoilt. He's had his way too much."

Rigdon squatted facing Ashe. "Go ahead, taste that brew, partner. It comes straight from Missouri."

Colby tasted it and nodded as he offered the pony to Rigdon, but the old man smiled and wagged his head. "Keep it. You'll likely need a nip off it now an' then. Mister Colby, it don't take long for a man to figure that losin' a little money is better'n getting buried, now, does it?" The sly old eyes brightened. "You'n me know that when it comes to thieving, you lose about as often as you win. Well now, I'm not sayin' anythin' terrible is goin' to happen to you if you don't cooperate, but like I just said, Joseph's big an' spoilt. He's also mean an' ugly when he's upset."

Colby believed that last sentence. "Mister Rigdon—"

"Call me Sid, just plain Sid."

"Sid, what I got cached is a hell of a long way from here."

"That's all right, son. It won't make no difference about that."

"And it's not six thousand dollars. . . ."

Rigdon's smile congealed.

"It's closer to ten thousand."

Rigdon's small eyes bored into Colby in apparent disbelief.

"An' it's cached in two different places, Sid. About half a month's ride from each other."

Rigdon had recovered quickly. "Five thousand in each place?"

"No. Seven in one place, three in the other. About three hundred miles apart."

"Well, I expect the thing to do would be to look up the seven thousand dollars first, wouldn't you say?"

Colby had another pull off the little bottle, then tucked it away. "Sid, it's over in New Mexico."

This time Rigdon's expression showed strain. "That's quite a ride, for a fact."

"Yes, it is."

"Where's the three thousand?"

"Down in Arizona near a place called Rosalia."

"I know the town well, Mister Colby. Been through there many times. Of course, that was years back, but towns don't change much, do they? Whereabouts, around Rosalia?"

"You know where the Arizona Rangers have a barracks down there?"

"Yes."

"About three miles due east from those barracks in a little canyon full of thornpin thickets."

"How come you hide it so close to the Rangers?"

Colby smiled. "A man couldn't find a better place, could he? Let them guard it for me."

Rigdon lightly scratched the tip of his nose about that. "Maybe."

"Sid? Men in our trade don't have much reason to trust one another, do they?"

The old man straightened up a little and gestured with both hands. "Son, I told you: You're a free man the minute we got our hands on the money. It's that money that'll guarantee you bein' alive for years to come. You can trust me, Mister Colby."

Colby was comfortably aglow as he sat relaxed, eyeing the old man. "Sid, what does a man do in a godforsaken place like this to make a living?"

Rigdon looked away and muttered, "There are things, son, there are things."

"I didn't see any cattle around here?"

"Well, no. We give up on ranchin' years ago."

"Mustanging?"

The old man was amused. He faced Colby and said, "I'm too old for that, an' my boys got no interest in ridin' themselves raw to catch a bunch of inbred, undersized, mean-as-catamount wild horses that after you catch 'em you got to just about give away an' lose money on every one."

Colby persevered. "You make whiskey?"

Rigdon shook his head. "We just limp along, as the feller said. Just sort of hang on, relyin' on the Good Lord to keep us from starving." Rigdon stood up. "I'll talk to the boys. Maybe, if you're fit to ride in a day or two, we can go after the money."

Rigdon did not forget to bar the door from the outside. Colby let his head ease back very gently against the wall. It was a wonder he wasn't dead, and he damned well might be yet, but right at this particular moment he felt better than he'd felt since he was ambushed. In Missouri they made pretty good popskull.

Someone pushed a slip of limp white paper under the door. Colby probably wouldn't have noticed it if the person beyond the door hadn't made little abrasive sounds as they got down to push the paper where he could see it.

He waited until he thought whoever had been out there had departed, then went over, got the slip of paper, and carried it to a sliver of light. In a childish hand with painfully round letters, someone had written, "They didn't find it but I did." Below that single line was the drawing of a star.

He wadded up the note, found a crack in the wood to force it into, and returned to his sitting place. Whoever had written that note had to be someone who'd had access to his saddlebags. He knew it wasn't the old man or his son Joseph. If they'd found the badge, they wouldn't still be after the money—and chances are they'd have shot Ashe Colby where he sat.

That left Samuel or his mother. But Colby doubted either one of them would write that note. Samuel appeared to be completely dominated by his brother. And the old man's wife wasn't the type to go out of her way to help a stranger, from what little of her Colby had seen.

"The lithe kid with the old hat!" He said it aloud, in a sudden revelation.

No one came for him when it was time for the midday

meal. He didn't have much appetite anyway after receiving the note, not even when dusk descended and Joseph and his brother came for him. He told them he'd just as soon skip supper. Joseph wrenched him to his feet and with his snarling face close, said, "You'll eat when we say so, but that's not all you'll do. We got to palaver. The old man told us what you said. We need more'n just talk, cowboy."

Joseph gave Colby a violent shove in the direction of the door. He nearly collided with Samuel before catching himself. No one said a word until they reached the kitchen—and Colby's breath stopped in his throat. The lithe youth was at the table between Rigdon and his wife. At Colby's puzzled look, Rigdon waved a hand. "This here is our youngest, our catch-colt."

Colby moved woodenly to a chair and sat opposite the "catch-colt." Hell, it wasn't a boy at all but a girl who, from a distance, looked like a boy. She had long, wavy hair. Up close, he noticed her flawless complexion, her even features, and the large gray eyes, like her mother's. The girl's gaze was fixed on Colby.

"Her name's Amilie," Rigdon continued. "Everybody calls her Lee. She's the one found your tracks and kept your attention while me'n the boys got up there behind you."

Colby nodded. Amilie did not respond at all, but she did not take her eyes off him except to eat. Old Rigdon was in a fine mood as he patted the girl's shoulders while talking about her. "She can rope as good as either of the boys, an' she can cook too." He slyly winked. "An' ain't no one better at baitin' a trap—but I guess I don't have to tell you that, do I, Mr. Colby?"

The girl was red as a beet as she looked at her plate. Without eating very much, she pushed the food one way, then another.

The old man was still fired up. "How old would you figure she is, Mister Colby? Go right ahead, spit it out, Amilie don't mind."

She obviously did mind. Her face was scarlet, her eyes were fixed on her supper plate, and both hands were lying in her lap below the table like wounded birds.

Colby looked from the girl to her mother, then at the old man's sons. Everyone but the old man's wife and the girl seemed to think this was a huge joke. Colby didn't. Aside from adding to the girl's anguish, the wrong answer could get him killed, if she had his badge in her pocket and got mad enough to fling it atop the table.

He said, "Hard to say when they're that pretty, Sid."

The old man hooted. "You're pretty good at weaseling, ain't you? She's eighteen an' looks fourteen. But one of these days she'll blossom out."

Joseph interrupted in his savage way. "That's enough." He was glaring straight at Ashe Colby. "Supposin' we ride all over hell and you give us the wrong directions?"

Sid Rigdon held up a hand, still smiling. "Not if he goes along, son, an' it wouldn't be worth the ride unless he did. You can see that, can't you?"

Samuel answered. "I can see that, Paw. When do we head out?"

The old man hung fire over his answer until there was absolute silence. "Well now, you both know someone's got to take the bundle out of here. I know it was Sam'l's turn, but something's come up that we got to adjust to. Me, I ain't up to ridin' all the way down to Arizona then over to New Mexico, so I'll deliver the bundle an' you boys can ride with Mister Colby."

Both Rigdon's sons stared at their father. If the old man read anything from this he did not allow it to show. He continued to smile and to eat his breakfast. As he was pulling the napkin from his shirtfront he said, "Just remember to come back, boys. We been a family for a long time. Ain't no amount of money, good or bad money, that can replace family, now, is there?"

Amilie and the woman abruptly arose to clear the table.

Both were tight-faced and silent, making a point of not looking at any of the men.

Burly Joseph arose, flung down his napkin, sucked his teeth while gazing at the old man, and finally jerked his head in the direction of the front porch. Sid and Samuel followed him to the porch, leaving the captive to sip coffee while straining to hear what was being said out there.

When Colby failed at that, he arose to help clear the table. Once, as he brushed against Amilie, she looked straight up into his face. He smiled. She turned back to her work and afterward was careful to keep something between them: either the table, a chair, or Rigdon's wife.

Mrs. Rigdon turned around, carrying a wet rag from the big dish basin on the stove. She looked steadily at Colby for a long moment, as though she either had something to say to him or perhaps because she hadn't as yet been able to make a judgment of him. But again, when he smiled, the woman turned her back to him.

The palaver out front took a long time. Colby was standing by a fire-blackened, big stone fireplace in the parlor when the old man returned. Rigdon walked over to a rack of antlers for a hat, which he dumped on the back of his head while looking at Colby. He said, "Well now, Joseph's worryin' that there ain't no caches, and that on such a long ride, you bein' coyote an' all when it comes to outlaw tricks . . . You understand what I'm gettin' at, Mister Colby? There's many a slip between the bowl an' the mouth, so to speak."

Colby replied reassuringly, "Sid, your boys will be armed. I won't. Joseph looks strong enough to fight a bear. The caches are down there."

Rigdon nodded. "An' somethin' else. I told 'em to take along a set of chains. Sam'l said that horse of yours looks like he could run a hole in the daylight." Rigdon smiled. "I told him ain't no horse been born that can outrun a bullet." Rigdon shrugged his thin shoulders. "Sam'l echoes his brother. Always has."

Rigdon leaned on the wall near the hatrack studying his prisoner. "Tell you what, Mister Colby. We bein' more or less in the same line o' work, I sort of wish we'd met different."

"Why?"

Rigdon shifted his stance and shot a rapid look over his shoulder before speaking again, in a softer tone. "Well, Joseph's been harpin' about leavin' the country. Takin' our profit an' maybe goin' out to California, or somewhere. But me, I grew up in the Wolf Hole country. So did Lizbeth. We got reasons to stay. Mister Colby, if you was my age with grown sons you'd know young fellers get a cravin' to ride on, to look around, to see things. They get restless."

"What's that got to do with me?"

The old man was having a struggle with himself. Caution won out, so all he added to what he'd already said was, "If Joseph goes, that dim-witted brother of his'll go too. An' I can't run the business by myself. . . . Well, I'd better lock you up. Walk down the hall ahead of me."

An hour later, sitting in near-darkness again, Colby rolled and lit a cigarette. He watched the smoke drift lazily upward and form a variety of shapes.

He'd ridden a month through purgatory in order to sneak up on the residents of the Wolf Hole country because there was no other way for a stranger to appear without being noted, only to ride straight into a damned ambush like a greenhorn. But unless the pieces he'd been putting together from the conversations of his captors lately were just so much smoke, he had stumbled into the very thing he'd been sent up here to locate: the den of the renegades whose activities were having serious consequences as far east as Missouri and as far west as California's lawless Barbary Coast.

CHAPTER 5

A Dangerous Riddle

IT was two days later, when old Rigdon took Colby down to the barn where Joseph was shoeing a horse, that the final discussion was held. Joseph did not trust Colby. In fact, Joseph Rigdon did not trust anyone except his brother Samuel because as they'd matured together, Joseph's domination had been so complete that not once since childhood had Samuel crossed Joseph.

Joseph worked hard, shirtless and sweating. His back was a smooth, glistening hide packed full of muscle. Colby hadn't been far wrong when he'd thought Joseph Rigdon could probably manhandle a bear.

Samuel was helping, shirtless too, sweat dripping as he trimmed for the shoes while Joseph ran the bellows on the forge. He also did the shaping at the anvil, and finally, the nailing. They worked very well as a team. There was no reason why they shouldn't have, they'd been working that way since their teens. Even when their father had groaned and moaned about his advancing age and how it robbed him of chances to do so many things he'd enjoyed doing as a young man, such as shoeing horses—which had to be a damned lie because no one in his right mind actually liked to shoe horses. Especially when the weather was as hot as the hubs of hell.

Joseph neither smiled nor nodded as his father and their prisoner went deeper into the shaded old barn to sit on up-ended horseshoe kegs. Joseph rhythmically pumped the forge bellows while eyeing them. As he released the handle

33

and moved to tong a homemade shoe into the fierce heat, his father said to him, "You figure to ride out in the morning, do you?"

Joseph withdrew the cherry-red shoe, eyed it, flipped it, and shoved it back as he replied without looking away from the fire, "The way things look now, yes."

"How about the shoes on his horse?"

That brought the smouldering eyes up. "I didn't look at 'em. If his horse needs a new set, let him make 'em. How about it, cowboy, can you do that?"

Colby nodded, peered around the barn looking for his horse, and saw him down near the doorless rear opening. The bay's head was over the half door, as the horse watched everything that was going on up near the front doorway.

Samuel wiped off sweat and grinned, leaning on the rump of a seal-brown horse with one of those remount necks. "Mister Colby, that's a mighty fine animal you got."

Colby smiled back. "We been together quite a while. I don't know whether he's satisfied or not, but I am."

Samuel laughed and leaned down to run a hand from hip to fetlock so the waiting horse would know his hoof was going to be raised.

Joseph withdrew the hot shoe, doused it in a bucket, then hoisted a hoof to burn it level. He was nailing when he said, "I wish to hell we had proof, Paw. That's one hell of a ride down an' back just on this subbitch's word."

Old Sid spread his hands palms down. "I expect we could forget the three-thousand-dollar cache and just go for the seven-thousand-dollar one. We can pick up the other later, anytime." The old man turned sly. "Maybe when we strike camp here an' head for California. It wouldn't be exactly on the way, but what the hell."

Joseph was nailing a hind shoe and looked around the animal's ham at his father. "Rosalia's on the way to California?"

"Sure it is, boy. Not exactly as the crow flies, but goin' a mite out of the way'd be worthwhile."

Joseph returned to nailing and clinching. He was rasping the finished hoof beneath the horse's belly when he spoke again. "I just wish to hell there was some way to make damned certain."

Again the old man spread his hands palms downward. "How, son? Mister Colby's word's got to be good. He knows as well as you do that if it ain't down there, he'll be tryin' to see the sky from beneath a cairn of grave-rocks, so why would he lie?"

"To stay alive," stated Joseph, and his brother chimed in.

"That's a fact, Paw," Samuel said. "To stay alive."

The old man ignored Samuel. So did Joseph as he finished rasping, moved out from beneath the raised hoof, and leaned across the animal's rump gazing at Ashe Colby. He said nothing, he simply wagged his head and led the shod horse to a stall and turned him in. After he came back he drank deeply from a dipper in the water bucket, watched his brother for a while, then crossed to the anvil and perched on it, eyeing Ashe Colby.

In anticipation of something disagreeable being said, Colby spoke first. "I was goin' to suggest to you, once we're on the trail, that there's one hell of a straight stretch of road between Rosalia and the cities easterly."

Joseph scowled. "What of it?"

"The bank at Rosalia gets all its operatin' funds from those easterly big city banks. It's delivered by stagecoach."

Old Sid laughed and struck his upper leg with one hand. "The man's got a business head on him, Joseph."

But his eldest son's scowl only grew darker when he responded. "You said last night there was a Ranger post in Rosalia, Paw."

Sid's expression changed. "That's right, Joseph. Best to forget about robbing any stages down there. Just get the seven thousand dollars and come home."

Joseph spat in disgust, watched his brother cross-tie the next horse to be shod, and kept his back to the seated men so long that Sid nudged Colby and led the way back out into the sunlight.

Colby returned to the house with Rigdon. There was no sign of Mrs. Rigdon or Amilie. Sid Rigdon fetched a whiskey bottle from a cupboard, placed it on the table, and pointed to a chair. Colby sat down.

After he drank from the bottle he lowered it and handed it to Colby. The old man said, "He's hard to get along with, Mister Colby."

Colby did not swallow, although he pretended to before putting the bottle between them as he spoke. "I got to tell you, Sid, I'm not lookin' forward to ridin' with him, an' I'm real uncomfortable what'll happen after I hand over the cache."

"Now, now. I told you; they'll turn you lose. Trust me, Mister Colby."

Colby made a funereal smile at the older man. "I'd like to be able to."

The women entered the kitchen from out back, saw the men at the table, and after putting two baskets on a counter, turned around and left the house the same way they'd entered it. Before Amilie left she had looked Colby squarely in the eye, but her face had remained expressionless. As he watched her leave the house, he wondered whether she would keep her secret until he, Samuel, and Joseph were on the trail. If she didn't, he'd never leave this place alive.

It was a hell of a thing to have a man's life dependent upon a linchpin like that flat-chested, leggy girl with a sprinkling of freckles across the saddle of her nose, and the ripe but down-curving, disillusioned mouth.

Colby's palms were wet when the old man picked up the bottle, tilted his head briefly, then placed it back between them as he spoke. "You ever run across any Arizona Rangers?"

Colby looked Rigdon straight in the eye when he replied. "A time or two."

"Must not have been up close. They got a reputation for shootin' first and askin' questions second. They've nosed around this country a time or two, but they're at a disadvantage. To get down here to the Wolf Hole country they got to come up into Mormon country, an' ride south. Well, sir, folks are real clanny in Utah. They got reasons for not carin' very much for Arizona law. Or U.S. law." Rigdon's color was improving by the minute. He smiled. "Or any kind of law."

He paused, then asked, "Where you from, Mister Colby?"

Colby's answer was factual. "New Mexico, over near the Texas line. My folks came from Indiana before I was born."

"Couldn't make it in Indiana, eh?"

"No one could over there, Sid. Unless they left off tryin' to raise corn and spuds an' whatnot on soil that wasn't more than three inches deep."

Rigdon eyed the bottle but made no move toward it as he said, "Same in this country. I ran five hunnert head of cattle. Never owned a fat cow in my life, an' what didn't pee blood from the drinkin' water in late summer an' die on me, the danged In'ians—or someone anyway—run off."

Colby nodded commiseratingly. "My paw used to say folks are born into grief too deep for tears and mostly they die in the same condition."

Sid's eyes came up off the bottle. "Your paw was a wise man. Tell me: Did he ever figure a way to make a decent living?"

Colby sensed where this conversation was leading, and lied to further it. "Yes. He rustled cattle, but when the bottom dropped out of the beef market, he still wasn't any better off. Except that by then the law was after him too."

Rigdon's gaze returned to the bottle. He was silent so long Colby had just about given up hope that he'd speak at all when he said, "Well, I better lock you in again," and raised his eyes to Colby's face. "If it wasn't for Joseph, I think you'n me could work something out."

He did not elaborate. As he'd done before, he jerked his head for Colby to precede him down the dingy hallway to the dark little room.

It was impossible to guess the time of day from that room, but Colby had learned to interpret sounds from deeper in the house. The women, for instance, made a recognizable sound when they put thick crockery plates on the table. They made a different sound when they were cleaning the house. One thing he noticed about them was that while they worked together, they rarely conversed.

He thought the day was well advanced when he heard Joseph and Samuel enter from outside. Colby figured suppertime wouldn't be far off, so he took one swallow off the little bottle Rigdon had given him, rolled and lighted a smoke, and thought about the ride south down to the Rosalia area.

They'd go eastward, which would be a blessing. Rosalia was somewhat in that direction, but even if it had been directly southward he did not believe the Rigdons would want to risk crossing the reservation the way he had, because by now springtime would be yielding to summer.

The rat returned. With his eyes adjusted to the gloom Colby saw that it was limping. His hurled boot must have connected after all. Colby moved his hat close to his right side, and for lack of anything else to occupy his time, he sat perfectly still watching the rodent. If it came within striking distance he intended to smash it with his fist.

A sliver of weak light that came under the barred door allowed Colby to watch the rat's movements. If that light hadn't brightened the floor for a short distance, he wouldn't have been able to see the rat, although he would still have been able to hear it.

His concentration was distracted when something beyond the door momentarily blocked out the light. The rat fled, which Colby did not notice as he turned his head slightly to watch a shadow moving where the light came and went. The light was completely blocked out for a scant moment before whatever had blocked it moved away, allowing the weak light to return.

Colby arose, moved silently toward the door, and picked up the scrap of paper which had been slipped under the door. He held it toward a sliver of sunlight that filtered through a crack in the west wall. But daylight was leaving. He had to get down on both knees and push the scrap of paper directly into the dying paleness, and even then he had difficulty making words out of the round scrawl.

In the end, he risked lighting a match. The note was less terse this time but just as troubling. "I left the steel mirror in the tree. If it was supposed to signal someone to help you, they'll never get here in time. There is a loaded gun under the old blankets in the corner. Don't use it here."

As before, he folded the note as small as he could and forced it into a crack. Then he stood listening, because he expected Joseph and Samuel to come for him at any moment. Although he was anxious to poke around in the filthy old blankets, he did not do so. Not for an hour and a half, by which time he'd been fed, growled at, and returned for the night to his prison.

There was a gun, as the note said, but when he held it up close to his face he had reason for disappointment. It wasn't what he'd assumed would be there: it was not a Colt six-gun, but was much smaller, a nickel-plated gun with a hammer that hinged to close forward and had to be hinged back to cock the gun. It was a double-action weapon and each pull on the trigger revolved the barrel for another shot.

It was loaded. The bullets were considerably smaller than .45 bullets. Colby guessed this was some variety of gambler's weapon. The hinged hammer would not catch in clothing when the weapon was drawn. Smaller caliber and double action signified the gun was for concealment in a pocket.

While it would certainly kill, with a shorter barrel than a regular six-gun had, the range wouldn't be very great.

He sighed. Beggars couldn't be choosers.

He hid the gun in the back of his waistband inside his shirt. He lit a smoke and stood in darkness for a long time wondering why she had done this. The first note hadn't been friendly. The second one hadn't been friendly either, it had simply stated facts and offered a warning. He was not to attempt to use the weapon while he was in the Rigdon's yard.

She had his badge, had evidently gone back to his camp to scout up the area, and had found his heliograph mirror. Apparently, she sneaked the gun into his prison while he and the other men were at the barn and while her mother was somewhere else.

She had taken a risk with that first note, but with the second one, and the gun, she'd put her life in as much danger as his own. Maybe more danger.

Old Rigdon's greed had kept Colby alive and probably would continue to do so until they discovered there were no caches. But Amilie was their own flesh and blood. What had been drummed into him before starting for this country was that these were very close, clanny, suspicious people. He had been told there would be no exceptions.

He killed the cigarette, went to make some kind of order of the blankets and bed down for the night.

But it seemed that there were exceptions, and if this was true, then evidently someone was serving a personal purpose in a very dangerous way.

CHAPTER 6

A Delay

BUT there was an interruption to the routine of the ranch shortly after breakfast the following morning when Joseph and his brother got their traveling gear and left it on the porch out front, then went back for a brief conference with their father.

When the Rigdons took Colby outside to get ready to leave, they noticed the appearance of three riders on the horizon. When Sid Rigdon saw them he acted like he'd been stung. He snapped at his sons, "Get them bedrolls and saddlebags out'n sight. Colby, go back to your room an' don't come out until one of us fetches you. And Mister Colby. Not a blessed sound. Not even a loud breath." Because Joseph and his brother were hustling their traveling gear toward a room in the east of the house, only Mrs. Rigdon and Amilie remained. They acted unnaturally stiff until the old man said, "You two herd Mister Colby to his room and lock him in. No—Lizbeth, you make some hot coffee. Amilie, you lock him in."

Everything happened so fast Colby's bewilderment remained with him until he and Amilie were at the doorway of his prison, then he turned with a wrinkled brow. "What is it? The law?"

She shook her head. "The elders. He don't want them to know anything about you. If they knew they'd scourge him sure as we're standin' here." She jutted her jaw to indicate that he should enter the room.

Instead of obeying, he looked closely at her. "Amilie, where did you get that little gun?"

"Just go inside. I got to go back."

He reached and held her by the arm. "Why?"

She wrenched free, glared and pushed him roughly backward, slammed the door, and dropped the bar into its hangers. He heard her hastening back toward the front of the house.

For a while the house was quiet before Colby heard heavy, booted footsteps enter from out front. He could hear masculine voices but could distinguish nothing that was said. He did, however, identify Sid Rigdon's voice from the others and thought, with a shake of his head, that old Sid had missed his calling. He should have been an actor. The old hypocrite's voice sounded as genial and calm as ever.

Whoever the visitors were, they appeared in no hurry to depart. They were still in the parlor when dinnertime arrived, which was probably not a coincidence. People who used horses to travel very far looked forward to, and expected, hospitality.

It was freely given, which was also the custom. But after the meal Colby thought the conversation was moving toward the porch. When he heard the door slam—a little louder than was necessary—he sat on the old blankets watching the sliver of light beneath the door.

The visitors wouldn't ride out today. Even though there was still plenty of daylight, they would lie over and strike out before sunrise tomorrow because that, too, was the custom.

He thought about the mysterious Amilie with the rocklike expression and the muscular build. All he could come up with had to do with what he assumed were violent dislikes of what her father and brothers did. Her mother, too, had that constant expression of leashed disapproval, but with Mrs. Rigdon it probably had become second nature to disaprove and to do nothing about it. With Amilie, rebellion simmered; otherwise she would have given them Colby's badge by now and she certainly wouldn't have provided him with that little gambler's weapon.

The door was opened suddenly. Joseph appeared in the doorway, the light at his back making him appear even thicker, more menacing, than he was. "On your feet," he snarled. After Colby had arisen, Joseph stood eyeing him for a while before speaking again. During that interval Colby's heartbeat grew fainter. The look on the other man's face could have meant that the Rigdons suspected who he was, or perhaps had been warned by those three visitors that a stranger was in their country.

He was wrong.

Joseph finally spoke. "I don't know why the old man believes you, except that maybe the pair of you was cut from the same cloth."

Colby relaxed a little. "The old man said it. No matter how much money a man's got, it's not worth dyin' over. Besides, I'll make it back."

Joseph's voice was cold when he said, "Pretty good at your trade, are you?"

Colby forced a bleak smile. "Good enough."

"Then what are you doin' up in this godforsaken country?"

"Taking cover."

Joseph appeared to turn this over in his mind, and to reluctantly accept it as the truth, because he shrugged thick shoulders and stepped aside as he said, "Walk ahead of me. We're goin' to the barn. Your horse's shoes is too thin to last long."

There was no one in the house as they passed through or, if there was, Colby saw no sign of them.

The heat was rising, the sun was halfway on its climb toward the meridian, there was no heat-haze yet, and the barn was pleasantly cool when he entered it to find his mule-nosed bay horse cross-tied for shoeing.

Colby ignored Joseph as he shed his shirt and hat, pumped

the forge bellows, and looked around for the steel. Joseph pointed to a long, curved rake tooth. Without a word Colby went to work. The teeth from a hay rake made better shoes than the soft steel of store-boughten plates. They lasted through three or four resettings.

Joseph sat on a little keg watching everything Colby did. While Colby was removing the bay horse's old shoes and trimming the hoof, Joseph rolled and lit a smoke. Not until Colby was punching nail holes in the finished shoes at the anvil did Joseph finally speak. His voice was less hostile for the first time. "You do some cowboyin', did you?"

Colby paused between strikes to reply. "My share, I guess, until I figured out it was damned hard work for the money an' took up an easier way to make a living."

Joseph dropped his quirley and ground it underfoot. "Like robbin' stages?"

"Yes, but that's a hit-an'-miss business. I must've scattered a ton of letters before I figured gettin' rich wasn't inside mailbags." Colby paused to smile ruefully at the burly man. "Some men figure things out early and some figure things out late. I'm one of the late ones. By the time I got the idea that to make money you got to go where it is, I was on everybody's wanted list."

Colby fitted the first shoe, clinched two nails before setting the other six, then straightened up to add a little more to what he'd already said. "Banks. That's where the money is. Banks. A friend of mine said railroad mail cars carryin' payrolls and bullion were best. Well, he walked right into the barrels of a Pinkerton sawed-off scattergun in Wyoming."

Joseph leaned forward, watching Colby set the clinches and rasp the outer hoof. "Pretty good job," he said dispassionately.

Colby set the next shoe with the silence between them dragging on until Joseph spoke again. "That scar across your shoulder . . . ?"

Colby continued to work as he said, "There's risk in any

business, I expect. A storekeeper saw me comin' out of a bank in New Mexico and let fly. He was shakin' like a leaf or he'd have got me through the heart."

"How much did you get that time?"

Colby raised up looking at Joseph Rigdon. "I don't like to recall that one. Three hundred dollars."

Joseph spat and shook his head. "Like you said, there's risks. How about the next time?"

Colby brightened. "Two thousand in greenbacks." He paused, looking straight at the other man. "Don't touch silver and don't take gold, unless you got plenty of time. They're too heavy. Greenbacks got no weight and you can carry as many as you can shove inside your shirt."

Joseph arose, went to the front barn opening, and leaned there squinting out across the empty yard for a moment or two, then turned and said, "Eat big tonight because Sam'l or I'll come for you before sunup in the morning." With that out of the way, the burly man continued to watch Colby work. He was thoughtful for a long time, then blew out a big, ragged sigh. "How many days you expect it'll take us to get down to Rosalia?"

Colby replied without looking up. Joseph had said nothing about a round trip. "Six, maybe eight. No more."

Joseph continued to stand in a slouchful silence for a while. Eventually, when he turned to study the yonder countryside again, Colby risked a question. "Where's your brother?"

"Out with the old man. They'll be back directly."

By the time Colby finished and put his animal back into its stall and forked it some woody hay that had been left to dry too long before being hauled in, Joseph was back on the little keg, whittling with a wicked-bladed claspknife that had horn handles.

He tossed the stick away and arose, pocketing the knife. As Colby came over for his shirt, Joseph said, "Maybe you brought trouble." He gestured toward the yard. "Those men who rode in this morning said they'd got word, from a settlement east of here called Short Creek, that the In'ians was sayin' four strangers crossed east of here about twenty miles headin' for St. George."

Colby stuffed in his shirttail. "What's St. George?"

"A town north of here about ninety miles. It's over the line in Utah. Those visitors told the old man they had scouts out watchin' for those four strangers. They said it was possible they could be lawmen."

Colby buttoned the shirt and strolled toward the front of the barn. "Lookin' for me? Is that what you're saying?"

Joseph nodded. "Maybe. Folks in this country keep an eye peeled for strangers. They've done it since the government sent an army against the Mormons when I was a baby."

Colby was about fifteen feet from the burly man, showing skepticism when he said, "Not for me, partner. There was no sign of anyone trailin' me, and anyway I came in from the west, not up north any ninety miles." Colby paused without taking his eyes off Joseph's face. "If it's lawmen, they're most likely comin' up here for some other reason. You got a bank in St. George?"

Joseph shook his head. "No, an' not much else. Let's get something to eat."

The subject languished between them until about half an hour later. They were finishing their meal, served by Mrs. Rigdon—there was no sign of Amilie—when Sid and Samuel rode in. The old man left his younger son to care for the horses and came across the yard beating off dust. When he walked in and saw Joseph and Colby at the table, he tossed aside his old hat and ignored them to address his wife. "Lizbeth, I'm hungrier'n a bitch wolf."

She said, "Sit down."

As the old man sank down he shook his head at Joseph. "I took 'em over there and give 'em the bundle." When Joseph barely nodded in understanding, Sid turned in the other direction. "You shoe your horse, Mister Colby?"

Colby nodded as the old man's wife placed a platter of

meat and potatoes on the table in front of him. Rigdon ignored them all until the edge had been taken off his hunger, then raised his head to ask where Amilie was.

Mrs. Rigdon answered shortly. "Out on the colt she's been breaking."

"She's been out a lot lately," complained the old man, returning to his meal.

His wife shot a waspish answer to that. "It was you told her to put a lot of sweaty saddle blankets under that colt."

The old man ignored the rebuke but held up an empty coffee cup, which his wife refilled. By the time the pleats were out of his gut, Rigdon reared back in contentment, asked if everything was ready for the departure tomorrow, and when Joseph said it was, the old man rolled his eyes around to Colby. "I feel real bad about takin' your savings," he said, "but you know how that goes, you'n us being more or less in the same business. So I been thinkin'. . . ."

Joseph's sulfurous gaze was fixed on his father. "Thinkin' what?"

"Well, the business could use another man, Joseph. Someone with the right qualifications an' all."

Joseph's retort was a complete surprise to Colby. He said, "You been long enough figurin' that out. All right—now what?"

"Well, son, you'n your brother'll still go get the money, but the three of you'll come back."

Colby wasn't surprised at this tacit admission that the plan had been to kill him down in Arizona, despite the old man's many reassurances that there was to be no murder.

Joseph, who had been watching his father, swung his attention to Colby briefly, then back to the old man. "All right."

Rigdon seemed relieved by that statement. "You're satisfied, are you?"

Joseph would not go quite that far. "Well, *if* we find the

cache an' the money's in it. What'n hell's keepin' Sam'l? He's been down there long enough to hatch a clutch of eggs."

Rigdon rolled his eyes. "You know your brother, a simple thing like washin' his face takes him longer'n anybody else. He'll be along. Maybe Amilie come back an' they're talkin' down there. Sam'l won't even know he's hungry until he walks in here an' smells cooking."

Rigdon laughed shortly. "On the way back he saw a bitch coyote with pups an' took off after 'em. I didn't see hide nor hair of him for two hours, then there he was, comin' up from the south on a sweaty horse, grinnin' like he had good sense."

The old man arose, ignored his wife, and jerked his head as he dropped the old hat back on his head. "Just in case he fell over his own feet, let's go down an' send him up to get fed."

Colby wasn't surprised at being included in this, and he was glad to be able to stand up because that damned little gun in his rear waistband gouged him harshly when pressed against the back of the chair.

The yard was shimmering in heat all the way to the barn, but it was pleasant inside. There was no sign of Samuel. Joseph jutted his jaw in the direction of a big roan colt eating its head off in a north-wall stall. The old man nodded. He'd already seen the colt. "I was right," he stated. "They're around here somewhere. Amilie's got that colt rode down to bone an' muscle."

They trooped through the dark barn toward the rear opening where the corrals were. Samuel and Amilie were out there in hot sunlight. They appeared to have been arguing. The old man waggled his head. "All right. Quit the damned janglin' an' go get somethin' to eat." He stopped speaking and stared at something in his younger son's hand. "What you got, boy?"

Samuel held it up with a proud smile. "She was tryin' to trade me out of it."

Colby's heart stopped for a fraction of a second. Samuel was holding up his steel heliograph mirror.

Joseph roughly shoved his father aside on the way toward his brother. He snatched the steel plate away, and while fiercely regarding it, snarled aloud. "Where'd you find this thing, Sam'l?"

"Well, I took off after some coyotes. They run like the wind and . . ."

Joseph's big fist closed over sweaty shirting as he wrenched his startled brother off the edge of the stone trough. "Where did you get this? I don't give a damn about no coyotes. *Where did you find this?*"

Samuel was too startled to reply immediately, so Joseph shook him the way a dog would shake a snake. The old man intervened. "Stop it! Joseph, let him go. Now then, Sam'l, where did you get that mirror?"

The unnerved younger man smoothed his shirt and shot a frightened look at his glowering brother when he replied. "I run them coyotes atop that ridge where we caught Mister Colby. I lost 'em when somethin' like to blinded me. It was that thing hangin' on a limb in a juniper tree."

CHAPTER 7

The Odd Partnership

COLBY was prepared—not for the suddenness of what happened, but he'd had sufficient time while the Rigdons were yelling at each other to reach around, palm the gambler's gun, pull back the collapsible hammer, and cock the weapon.

When the old man and Joseph turned slowly it was quiet enough to hear a crow squawking in flight some distance away. Colby spoke crisply. "Amilie, saddle your horse and mine. *Move, girl!*"

She moved, passing wide around the three Rigdons. As she entered the barn, her father wagged his head. "Mister Colby, you're a real disappointment to me. We was just beginning—"

"Use your left hands to lift out those guns and drop them," Colby told the brothers. "You too, Sid." When the Rigdons didn't move at his order, Colby tipped the little gun until it was aimed squarely at the broad chest of Joseph. *"Now!"*

Samuel recoiled from the sharpness of the command and fumbled to disarm himself. The old man was next. Joseph stood like a stone, eyes narrowed and fierce. Colby waited a moment before saying, "You think I won't do it? You got two seconds. You'll never hear the gun go off."

Rigdon interceded in a whining tone. "Do it, boy. Drop it like he says. He'll kill you."

Joseph dropped his weapon. As it struck the dust he said, "I told you, Paw. I warned you the night we first locked him up."

Colby listened to the sounds behind him where the girl

was rigging out horses. He gestured for the unarmed men to step back. As he retrieved their handguns without taking his eyes off them, Rigdon used his most persuasive voice to convince Colby he was making a terrible mistake. "We'll just forget this. Won't we, boys? Mister Colby, you'd fit in real good with us. It'll pay better'n robbin' banks an' there ain't no risk. None at all. Now then—"

"Shut up," Colby said. "Turn around. Your backs to me. *Do it!*"

Joseph and Samuel obeyed, but the old man spread his hands. "Now then, Mister Colby, don't do somethin' that's goin' to rouse up the countryside. We got an awful lot of friends down here. One gunshot'll carry a long ways."

Colby stepped closer, aimed at a spot between the old man's eyes, and repeated his command. "Turn around!"

The old man obeyed. He was the first to be struck across the head. As he was falling Joseph started to turn, not soon enough. There was the sound of steel over bone as Joseph's eyes rolled up and his knees turned loose. Samuel too was beginning to turn, and again, not quickly enough to avoid the gun barrel.

Colby leaned to examine each man closely before returning the big six-gun he'd used to his waistband. Behind him Amilie's voice was pitched as high as a child's when she said, "Are they dead?"

He turned. "No. Hurry up with that saddling."

She jumped to comply.

Colby went to the front of the barn to look in the direction of the house. There was no sign of Mrs. Rigdon. He also studied the empty, heat-hazed land to the north and east before turning to Amilie, who pressed a pair of reins into his hands as she said, "They'll be after us."

Before he took the reins he freed every stalled horse. "If they come after us, they'll have to sprout wings," he told her, gesturing for her to get astride her colt. From the saddle she watched him yank loose britches-belts to lash the ankles and wrists of the unconscious men, use their bandanas to gag them. As he stood up, he looked into her white face and handed back the little gun she'd provided him with. He said, "Now you listen to me. And don't argue. We're goin' straight south."

Her eyes widened as her lips parted. "There's no water. Besides, that's the reservation an'—"

"Amilie, I said don't argue."

He swung astride, reined around the inert bodies in the barn, rode out, and turned southward. On the way past the house he watched for sign of Mrs. Rigdon. Amilie said, "She's makin' bread today," as though that meant she wouldn't be watching the yard.

They had two canteens Amilie had slung from their saddlehorns, but no food. The heat punished them for four hours as they rode. Even after the sun finally left, the heat remained—released from the earth, the rocks, even the sparse underbrush after being stored throughout the day.

Amilie watched him from the corners of her eyes, but did not volunteer another protest until they were riding through a cooling late night. Then all she said was: "This is hopeless. We should have gone east. I know that country. We could have hid by day. I know where the water is over there."

"I told you not to argue," he said, then reined back to stop and listen. If there was anyone behind them, they were too distant to be detected, although by now the Rigdons would certainly have got free and would have had enough daylight left to start tracking the fugitives. As they were moving again, Amilie reined over close and held out a hand that clutched something. She said, "Take it."

He took the badge, dropped it into a shirt pocket, and gazed at her.

"They dumped everything out of your saddlebags and left. I picked around. The badge was hooked into the seat of your extra pair of drawers." She looked quickly away and he laughed at her. All that accomplished was a heightening of the color in her face, which was not visible to him in the darkness.

"Where did you get that little gun, Amilie?"

"It belonged to my father."

He softly scowled. "Sidney?"

"No. My father. Mister Rigdon always said I was his catch-colt, but it wasn't true." She turned toward him again. "My father was a gambler. I don't know how he and Mister Rigdon met, but I remember that after they rode away one time when I was small, Mister Rigdon rode back leading my paw's horse with all his things on it." She looked away again. "They wouldn't say anything except that my paw'd just gone off by himself. When I was little I believed that. But later I knew different. No one survives on foot in this country. Not even Indians. Anyway, he never came back for me."

"What about your mother?"

"I never knew my maw, an' he didn't like to talk about her. We moved all the time, from town to town. Whatever he had, the Rigdons destroyed. Except for that little gun. I got that before they could destroy it. I hid it and kept it."

"Amilie . . . ?"

She turned fiercely on him. "No! I don't want to talk about it."

"The Rigdons raised you?"

"Missus Rigdon did, but we was never close, except that the last few years she did keep Sam'l and Joseph away from me. Now I don't want to talk about it no more. Do you know where we're going? You know, every year people die down in the desert an' when folks find their bodies they're dried out harder'n jerky?"

He looped the reins, rolled and lit a smoke, unlooped the reins, and rode in silence for miles, until the coolness made him suspect dawn was not far off. Then he abruptly altered course, heading for one of those ancestral camps he'd used on his way into the Wolf Hole country.

She studied him quizzically. "Do you know where you're going?"

He shrugged. "I sure hope so. Amilie . . . ?"

"What?"

"Well, nothing."

"I'll guess. I've already guessed part of it from that badge. You're after them, and like a fool I let them use me to catch you."

He smiled. "Go on."

"Well, how did you know what they're doing?"

"Sooner or later," he told her, "anyone who does what they've been doing on a large scale makes folks suspicious."

"How did you know it was them?"

"I didn't. Not until I'd been captured. Then it was little things they said." He abruptly stopped and looked at her. "You helped them."

She didn't deny it. "Now and then, yes."

"Who did you deliver the bundles to?"

"Those three men who rode in when I locked you in your room."

"Who are they?"

"All I know is that they'd be waiting by an old cottonwood tree about ten miles north of the ranch. I'd hand them the bundle, they'd say 'thank you' and that was the end of it. They rode north an' I rode back to the ranch."

"You don't know their names?"

"No, an' until they rode into the yard, I'd never seen them at the ranch."

"But you knew what was in the bundles."

She nodded. "I been out to the soddy where they make it, but they never let me inside." She looked over at him. "It's not just them, Mister Colby. I don't know who-all's in it with them, but I think it's a lot of folks. And they'll be scatterin' over the countryside come sunup lookin' for us."

He stuck to the point of his questioning. "Did you ever open a bundle?"

She sounded indignant when she replied. "No, of course not. What do you think I am?"

"A pretty girl," he replied, then pushed out more businesslike words. "It was counterfeit money. Hundreds of dollars' worth of it. Enough to cause problems all the way back east and as far west as California."

She rode silently beside him.

"Amilie . . . ?"

She faced him. "Mister Colby, unless you know a lot more about this country than I think you do, they're goin' to overtake us in a few days and bury the pair of us. If they don't, the desert will."

"Miss Rigdon . . ."

"Don't call me that. My name's Amilie Prescott."

"All right. Miss Prescott—"

"I'm used to just plain Amilie."

He nodded gravely at her. "An' I'm used to just plain Ashe."

"Is that your real name?"

"Yes. Ashe Colby."

"I thought when men like you—sheriffs and Arizona Rangers an' all—were on a trail, they used other names. To sort of throw people off."

"They do. I didn't think it was necessary this trip. Amilie, did you hear those men who rode in talking with Sid?"

"Yes. They said they thought four lawmen were coming up out of Arizona to cross back down into the Wolf Hole country by way of St. George, an' they'd warned some folks up there to watch for them—an' sock them away if they was really lawmen."

Colby rolled and lit a smoke, rode silently for a while before saying, "We're goin' back, Amilie. . . . I wish you weren't with me."

"Well, I am, an' if you think I'm afraid of trouble . . . Mister Colby, I've never had anything but."

"Call me Ashe. Just plain Ashe."

"I've had trouble since I was very small. I can take care of myself."

He smoked, eyed her askance, and asked if she'd ever fired that little gun.

She hadn't, but she'd fired other weapons: carbines and handguns. "They'd take me hunting with them after ruttin' season. They let me shoot, but mostly they took me'n Elizabeth along to skin an' gut what they killed. . . . Ashe, where are we?"

"Goin' east. There's a road over there, isn't there?"

"Yes, but they'll be watchin' that road like eagles, and sunup's on the way."

"I know that. We're goin' to turn north about a mile or two from the road. I need you to tell me where that damned road is and when we'd ought to turn north."

Her eyes were large on him. "North? Back up into the Wolf Hole country?"

"Yes."

She stared at him until he smiled at her. "Amilie, you know that country up there. This time they won't ambush me—us. You can see to that, can't you?"

"Maybe. Most likely, but why go back?"

"Because that mirror you an' Sam'l found was my signal to other lawmen where I was, and I left it there so's they could set their course by it."

She pondered that for about a mile, then, instead of asking more questions, she concentrated on the streaky sky to the east as she said, "But you're overlookin' one thing. Come daylight they can track us, an' sure as hell they will."

"You know the country."

"Ashe, sure I know the country an' they know how well I know it, but the point is that no matter where we go, all they got to do to kill us is keep on the tracks."

"It's rocky country, Amilie. Do you know where there are any patches of pure rock atop the ground? Or a good creek we can ride up the middle of?" He stood in his stirrups to look around and sniff the air. Dawn was close. He sat down as she answered his question.

"I might know a place, but we got to change course, ride more nearly northwest, an' that's in the direction they'll be comin' from." She looked at him. "I got a feelin' we're goin' to get ourselves killed."

He snorted. "Tell me that tonight, not right now. And those possemen comin' down here aren't the four men those other counterfeiters warned Rigdon about."

"They're not? Then who are they? They're lawmen, aren't they?"

"Yes. Arizona Rangers. But they aren't carrying badges. They'll say they are rangemen heading north in search of work." At her baffled look he told her the rest of it. "The real possemen will come in from the opposite side, from the west. If we can get back up there, we can be their eyes. You understand?"

She did an unexpected thing. She laughed at him. "You look real serious."

He rolled his eyes. "I am real serious. I want the Rigdons an' anyone else connected with them. An' I want you to show me where the soddy is where they print that money. Amilie, there's a reward. You can have it. Three thousand dollars."

She gaped at him. The most money she'd had in her entire eighteen years was five silver cartwheels. She still had them; at least she'd left them among her personal, private things back at the Rigdon ranch. She could no more conceive of three thousand dollars than she could take her eyes off him, until he also said, "I still wish I was alone." Then her expression underwent a complete change.

"Men! Just once I'd like someone to treat me like a person."

He considered her flat-chested, lean, sinewy, leggy frame and smiled to himself. "Right now I'd like to think of you as a scout who knows the country."

She glared at him.

CHAPTER 8

A Bad Moment

THERE was no question about Amilie knowing the country.
Just short of sunrise she led him to a prehistoric lava-rock
blister that had burst millions of years earlier to form a large
cave, large enough to admit ten horsemen. There was evidence in the accumulated, dusty debris underfoot that men
as well as various creatures had holed up here over the
millenia, leaving behind tiny broken bones, ancient char, and
a coating of smoke blackness on the ceiling and walls.

It was still in use as a habitation. Colby left the horses with
Amilie and prowled farther back where darkness grew
deeper. He encountered a ball of intertwined snakes, perhaps as many as thirty of them. He made no attempt to
count. Even though it was too dark to see them, the rattling
sounds identified the species for him.

He went back where Amilie was waiting and told her about
the rattlesnakes. She was frightened, which did not surprise
him very much, although she'd lived most of her life in
rattler country and surely must know by now that rattlesnakes, unlike human beings, warned potential enemies before attacking.

Sunshine penetrated partway into the cave. Amilie went
out front to scale the prehistoric blister-rock. When she
returned she said, "There's dust to the west, comin' down-
country."

Early-day visibility was best in desert country. He nodded
to himself. "How far north?"

"Quite a ways. But they're trackin' us sure as hell."

He looked at her. She swore as easily as men swore, evidently thought it was a perfectly natural method of expression and did it easily and casually. He decided they could discuss that another time; right now he drank from the canteen and urged her to do the same. It wasn't an altogether satisfactory substitute for breakfast, but it was better than nothing.

He said, "I'll tell you something, Amilie: As long as fugitives keep moving, whoever's after them is always behind them. If we stay hidden in here, we'll lose time and our trackers will eventually close the distance."

She understood. "All right. There's a haunted arroyo over closer to the road a mile or so. If we can get down in there without being seen, we can ride north where there's water and tree-shade."

He eyed her. She really did know the country. Not only that, but she accepted their fugitive status without batting an eye. He grinned as he said he was beginning to like her and she fired back at him: "I can't say the same for you today. Yesterday I could have, though."

His brows shot up. "What's different today?"

"You have whiskers today. They make your face look dirty. And why don't you throw a couple of those guns away? You look like a pirate with 'em stuck in your britches."

He followed her in the direction of the distant stage road through a blessedly cool, very early morning. Several times he rode sideways, looking for the dust banner she'd mentioned. He did not see it until Amilie was riding up a low swale. From that slight elevation he saw it. Their pursuers were still on the southward leg of their ride.

Amilie quartered until she found a deeply worn game trail, then reined down it with Colby three or four yards to the rear.

The arroyo was deep, with a trickle of muddy, warm water flowing southward down its middle. There were some trees down there, flourishing underbrush, even some berry bushes. The horses drank deeply and were left to browse as Colby and Amilie climbed back up the crumbly trail to watch the dust. Now the riders were nearing the end of the southward trail. Soon they would turn eastward. Colby sighed and looked at his companion.

"They'll see our dust too. The air's getting dry over here."

She surprised him again. "Over close to the road is a lot of rock." She faced him and smiled. "You know anything about the Navajo?"

He had to admit near-ignorance. "Only what I've heard. A little is all. Why?"

"Because I've known some of them. They're good at something like this. Come along, the horses are tanked up. I'll show you."

He watched her squirm around to descend the game trail.

Hell, she was enjoying this, empty gut and all. He traipsed after her down where it was cool and shady. The reason he hadn't wanted her along was based on what little he knew about females; they were bewildered when they were out of their own world. They complained and cried and brooded. They tired easily and were a burden.

She stopped where they could see the horses eating and waved her arms. "Haunted," she told him. When he put a disgusted look on her, she scowled back. "Indian spirits live here."

"You ever see any, Amilie?"

"You don't see 'em, Ashe, you feel 'em and sometimes you hear 'em."

"Have you been down here before?"

"Lots of times when I was breaking colts." She regarded his expression of skepticism and reddened a little. "You don't have to believe. Come along, we can ride out the upper end to flat land and head for the rocky country."

The arroyo was about two miles long, brushy most of the way with an occasional tree. Once, they started up a band of antelope. The fleet animals went straight up the earthen sides of the canyon and disappeared in minutes. Another time they rode past a dilapidated, very old hogan. Here, she gestured. "Old Indian died there. He's one of the haunts."

Colby rolled and lit a smoke.

Near the upper end of the canyon she led him through thickets so dense and low he had to ride with one arm in front of his face as he crouched over the saddlehorn. Where they broke clear, a wide game trail led upward. Without hesitation she started up it. When they crested the top-out she halted, sat twisted in the saddle waiting until he was up there, then grinned at him.

He grinned back as she rode easterly. When the stage road was in sight, they were in rocky country. She turned northward.

They stirred no dust in this place, but far back there was dust rising. Colby made a guess to himself. There were at least three pursuers back there, and perhaps twice that many. But they were still a long away off.

Amilie stepped to the ground only once, when a rocking stagecoach and four went past in a loose gallop, raising enough dust to have been a company of cavalry. When it was far ahead, Colby wagged his head behind her back. She was not only enjoying this but she was good at it. His respect increased a little.

Where they halted again was well clear of the arroyo, with the ground sloping gradually on the east side of a bluff that dropped away abruptly to the west. He said, "That's where I hung the mirror."

She nodded while studying the roundabout country. When she spoke, she was staring intently up where thick brush obscured the lower elevation of the barranca. She quietly asked a question that made the hair arise on the back of his neck.

"Those friends of yours that're coming in from the west— could they be this far east by now?"

He didn't know whether they could be or not. "Why?"

"Because there are two horses tied in that big brush clump. Watch. They swing their tails."

She was right, but several minutes passed before he saw the movement. Whoever had left those horses had deliberately concealed them. He didn't think it could be the oncoming possemen from the west and said so. Amilie slumped in the saddle for a moment, then straightened up as she began reining around. "It would help like hell if we knew who was who out here."

They retraced their tracks for a mile, then started a big half-circling ride that would keep them hidden from whoever was atop the barranca. When he asked where they were going, she answered shortly. "I don't know. Just away from here. North, I guess." She squinted. "Why didn't you just get the soldiers to do this?"

"Because the army don't buy into local legal matters."

She looked scornful but said nothing. When they were well clear of the barranca, with Amilie doing as an Indian would have done—keeping plenty of distance and ground cover between whoever was up there atop the barranca watching for movement and themselves—she said, "I hope we can make the cache."

"What cache?"

"Where I have some tins of peaches and tomatoes and a bag of jerky. Aren't you hungry?"

"Yes. Amilie, how'd you come to have a grub-cache out here?"

"I told you; when I'm workin' a colt I make it cover lots of distance. I've got four caches, but this is the only one close by."

His respect for her went up another notch.

Her cache was in a stand of juniper brush. They had to lead their horses, otherwise someone watching would have been able to see them sitting astride. And they may have anyway.

The cache was shoulder-high in some gray rocks that

Nature's caprice had stacked one atop the other as though to create a wall. It looked enough like something human beings had created to have been such an edifice.

She was standing on tiptoe with her back to him while he held the horses when she said, "Lucky this time. I've had my caches ransacked by varmints a few times. That's why I made this one up the front of these rocks."

The horses were satisfied to stand with loosened cinchas and enjoy the shade while the man and girl sat at the base of the rocks eating. She watched him for a moment, then asked a question. "Are you married?"

It startled him. They were somewhere inside a surround of manhunting enemies and she was curious about his marital status. Women!

"No, ma'am. An' I don't ask personal questions either."

She accepted the rebuke as long as her mouth was full, but afterwards she said, "It's a woman's right. We're out here alone together an' a woman's got a right to know—"

He glared. "Amilie, damn it all, we're up to our armpits in bad trouble, woman's right got nothing to do with it."

She became silent so long Colby felt slightly ashamed for having been angry with her. To ameliorate things, he smiled at her. "Best food I've ever had."

She put a still-resentful look upon him. "I don't much care for men. Never have an' most likely never will."

He abruptly held up a hand. He was watching the nearby horses. Both the mule-nosed bay and her rawboned big colt were standing like statues, heads up, ears pointing, eyes fixed upon something Colby could not see because it was somewhere behind the rock pile at their backs.

He arose, drying both hands on his trousers. She came up beside him. He turned, shook his head, and whispered, "Stay here."

He handed her one of the six-guns from his waistband and began a stealthy creep around the rock pile to the north. The horses had not moved. They had to have noticed Colby's movement but were too engrossed with whatever was beyond his sight to even flick a glance in his direction.

He came to the edge of the rocks. They arose a good four feet above his head but ended very abruptly where he was standing motionless trying to detect sound.

One of the horses finally turned its head slightly to the left. The other one continued to stare eastward down the far side of the pile of balancing rocks.

Colby lifted the six-gun from his waistband, let it dangle at his side, and leaned as far as he could to peer around the side of the rocks. He was in this off-balance position when a steely voice spoke from northward and slightly westerly where one of the horses was staring.

"Drop the gun!"

Colby froze, hand tightening around the six-gun's grip.

"You drop it, or so help me I'll kill you!"

Colby wanted to lean back to straighten up, but the unseen man's last order had rung with promise. He opened his fingers, let the gun drop, then straightened back.

A dusty, faded-looking, gaunt man came up to his feet above where both horses were now staring. His old hat did not cover the mass of untidy and unshorn hair that grew low across his forehead and even lower at the temples. He was weathered to a light shade of dark mahogany. The gun in his right fist was aimed belt-buckle high and cocked. The man only had to flex the finger inside his trigger guard to keep his word about killing, when he raised his voice slightly. "Jack, I got him around here."

The answer came from alongside the pile of rocks where Colby had been about to lean for a look. "Did he drop it?"

"Yeah."

The second man, equally rawboned and sun-browned, stepped away from the rock wall, gun raised but not cocked as he walked to where he and Colby were separated by no more than thirty feet. He smiled wolfishly. "Well, well. Don, you was right, they did head back up here. Them damned fools down yonder'll be hours durin' the hottest part of the day ever gettin' up here."

The first man remained north of the horses, watching Colby when he said, "Hunnert dollars for him, partner."

The man with the cruel smile laughed. "Ol' Rigdon'll be glad to make it two hunnert."

Colby had been following this exchange while studying the two men. He'd never seen either of them before, but he'd seen many men just like them. They would kill. While he was watching them, a slightly breathless voice spoke from behind the second man.

"Throw away those guns!"

Colby's heart missed a beat. She had not obeyed him, she had slipped around the far side of the rock pile and was now in position behind the second man, whose face had suddenly lost every vestige of triumph.

"I'll break your spine from back here," Amilie said. "You over yonder near the horses: I can gut-shoot you before you can duck into those bushes. *Throw them down!*"

The man whose back was to Amilie said, "For Chris'sake, Don, you said she wouldn't still be with him."

Colby picked up his gun, cocked it, and pointed it at the man in front of the brush near the horses. "You got two seconds."

Both men dropped their weapons.

Colby moved around the rock pile, saw Amilie back there, holding the big gun he'd handed her with both hands, pointing it squarely at the nearest stranger's back. He sighed, shoved the stranger around in front of the rocks, gestured for the second man to cross over there too, then he wagged his head at Amilie. She lowered the gun and leaned against the rocks, white to the hairline.

CHAPTER 9

Questions and Answers

THE captives, along with being raggedy, threadbare range-men in need of soap, shearing, and shaves, were sullen toward their captors and each other. Don, the man with rusty light hair, continued to lean against the rock wall after Colby had ordered them both to sit down.

The other one, the man who'd been near the horses and whom his partner had called Jack, sat down immediately. He heeded Colby less than he did Amilie, and she did not like the way his eyes followed her every move.

Colby eyed the rawboned, lanky Don, whose thumbs were hooked in his shell-belt. Don gazed steadily at Ashe Colby in defiance of the order to sit down.

Colby repeated the order. Jack, who looked from one of them to the other, tugged at his partner's britches, but Don continued to stand.

Colby reset his hat, eyed them both, then methodically placed his weapons at Amilie's feet. Just as methodically, he put his hat beside them and started forward.

Don continued to slouch until the very last moment before pushing up off the wall, springing his knees a little, and raising rock-hard, bony fists. He was smiling.

Colby shuffled sideways, less to force Don to turn in order to face him than to draw Don away from his seated partner. He was partially successful, but if Colby closed with him, his seated partner would still be close enough to grab a trouser leg.

There was total silence until Amilie cocked a six-gun. The

sound was deadly in the stillness. Colby stepped back and looked around. She was pointing her cocked weapon at Jack, her purpose abundantly clear: If he moved a finger to help his partner she'd shoot him.

Don spoke scornfully. "Don't worry, girl, I don't need no help."

He was wrong, but just barely so. When Colby started forward again Don sprung both knees, catapulted directly ahead, and swung a roundhouse strike that grazed the side of Colby's head.

It was a good maneuver. If the blow had connected with Colby's jaw, the fight would have been over. But Colby had seconds to spin away, so the fist only grazed him. But his belly-blow with his turning body in behind it jackknifed Don. A sound like exploding air came from the man's mouth. He fell writhing, mouth wide open, eyes bulging in glassy shock.

Colby retrieved his hat, dropped it on, felt the slight swelling above his temple as he walked over and dispassionately dragged the gagging man over beside his friend and slammed him against the rock in a sitting position. He ignored Don and looked icily at Jack. "When I tell you boys to do something, be a good idea if you'd do it. Understand?"

Jack nodded his head.

As Colby walked over where Amilie was still holding the gun, Jack worried about his partner, who was just now beginning to get his breath back.

Colby gently took the cocked gun from the girl, eased the hammer down, and handed it back with a little crooked smile. She said, "Good thing I didn't stay in front of the rocks like you told me to do."

He gazed at her in silent exasperation, dropped down facing their prisoners, and asked Jack a question. "Who are you?"

"Well, just riders is all."

Colby nodded slightly. "Sure. You wouldn't lie to me, would you? How did you know we were over here?"

Jack gestured. "We was set to watchin' from up yonder where you'd hung a steel mirror. I saw you passing back an' forth through the easterly underbrush, but I didn't see her."

The injured man gasped out a bitter statement. "You damned fool, you knew there was two of 'em."

Jack did not face his friend, he continued to look straight at Colby. "I knew what the old man said. I also knew I saw only one rider." He finally turned to face his companion. "It was you said she bein' a woman an' all, she'd have dropped back somewhere an' he'd have abandoned her."

Colby stopped their bickering with a growl. "Who do you ride for?"

Jack's answer was preceded with that word he seemed unable to begin a statement without using. "Well, we don't ride for nobody regular. We work around the countryside. Mostly for some of the elders."

Colby drilled Jack with a stare. "Counterfeiting?"

Even suffering Don's eyes got round. Neither of them confirmed nor denied it, but Don's look of astonishment passed first. He said, "Who'n hell are you, mister?"

Instead of replying, Colby dug out the little badge and held it in plain sight on his palm. Don, who was holding his stomach with both arms, let his breath out in a rush and flicked an alarmed look at Colby. "Hell, they're keepin' watch up north. Where are the other three riders?"

"What other three?" Colby asked as he returned the badge to his shirt pocket.

"There was four of you comin' north up the stage road pretendin' to be rangemen. It didn't fool nobody. Where . . . how in hell did you—?"

Don, whose mind evidently worked faster, swore. "Damn. He couldn't have been one of them four, Jack. Old Sid said he caught him more'n a week back. You know what that means, for Chris'sake? Them four was to draw attention away from somethin' else." Jack rolled his eyes. "Partner, if them four are Rangers, an' so is this one, you know what I think? I think the damned country's likely swarmin' with Rangers. They fooled everyone an' we're smack-dab in the middle of a trap, sure as hell."

Don's middle seemed to have stopped hurting. He looked at Colby from a puzzled face, and Colby did nothing to brighten their mood. He smiled at them, sat down beside Amilie, shoved back his hat, and waited a moment before asking another question. "How'd you happen to be atop that barranca? Our tracks led southward."

Don replied, "The old man sent five down your trail and sent us over here, figuring you might be crazy enough, or scairt enough, to try backtracking."

"Where are the others? The old man and his boys?"

"Well, they're . . . they got somethin' else to do."

Colby smiled thinly again. "Clean out the soddy?"

Don refused to reply. So did Jack until Colby unwound up off the ground and removed his hat as he advanced on them. Then Jack squirted words in a rush. "Clean out the soddy an' get everythin' up to St. George where folks'll hide it where no lawmen'll ever find it."

Colby halted. "How many folks are involved in this counterfeiting business?"

Jack made an all-encompassing gesture with both arms. "Everybody. Even the ones who don't hold with it protect the others. Once or twice some upstandin' folks raised hell. They disappeared. Mister, this is a starve-out country. A man does whatever he's got to do to keep alive. Counterfeitin' has put money in everyone's pockets for the first time since we been down here." Jack was regaining his confidence. He showed his teeth as he said, "You better have an army with you. What you done to the Rigdons, and her runnin' off with you knowin' what she knows, has got the whole territory either out huntin' you or gettin' ready for war."

Don took courage from his partner's new attitude and added his two bits' worth. "You'n her will never get out of here alive, not even if you sprout wings. Riders'll be scourin' around from over as far as the Short Creek settlement, from Lee's Ferry, an' from up north in Utah around St. George. You kicked a hornet's nest this time, mister."

Colby stood regarding them in silence until Amilie spoke behind him. "Who's at the ranch?"

Both prisoners swung their attention to her, but only one answered. "Sid's old woman." As the implication of what he'd said sank in, the man also said, "That whole countryside up there'll be swarmin' with riders lookin' to shoot you'n him on sight."

Colby moved back and motioned for Amilie to stand up. While she watched, he retrieved the guns their captors had dropped, emptied them, then struck each weapon with violent force against unyielding granite and flung them aside. Don and Jack gazed unhappily at their ruined handguns.

As Colby approached the prisoners, Amilie's hands flew to her mouth and her eyes got perfectly round. But this time he did not knock them unconscious, he simply roughly hurled each man face down and left them tied at the ankles and with wrists lashed in back.

Amilie's composure returned as Colby asked where the men had left their horses; when they told him, he jerked her head for her to bring in their own animals. He did not say five words as they were riding away from the straining men in front of the balancing pile of rocks.

They located the horses, found food and canteens, appropriated both, dumped saddles and bridles on the ground, hoorahed the horses into free flight, and were riding again when Amilie said, "There wouldn't be any point in headin' for the ranch, would there?"

He was chewing jerky and was unable to reply for a long time. Saliva mixed with pepper-cured, shriveled, dried meat made the stuff swell in a man's mouth until conversation became difficult.

But eventually he answered her. "Nope. But I'd like to see that soddy."

She scowled at him. "You heard them say there wouldn't be anything left."

He was chewing again. He was also riding with a thoughtful crease in his forehead between the eyes. She had to be satisfied with this expression of thought until she abruptly halted and raised a hand. "Did you see that flash?"

"No, what direction?"

"Up there. Northwest."

He looped both reins and fished for the makings. Under her steady gaze he twisted up a smoke, lit it, and spat flakes of tobacco off his tongue. Then he smiled at her. "I'd say it's maybe a little more'n fifty-fifty that this time it's not enemies. Amilie, they've had enough time by now to get here, comin' in from the west."

"Ashe, that was *northwest*. That was upcountry."

He nodded about that, still looking in the direction she'd seen the heliograph signal. "Tell me something, partner: Do these folks down here ever use heliograph signals?"

She shook her head. "I don't think so. Leastways I've never heard of 'em doin' it. Why should they? They've never had a real organized challenge to face before. Like that feller said back yonder, the one you knocked the breath out of, this whole territory down here an' up into Utah, too, is part of the same goddamned conspiracy."

He trickled smoke, gazing at her. She reasoned like a man, but by now he knew her better than to think she would take that as a compliment. She'd be all over him like a rash. He blew out a big breath, killed the cigarette atop his saddle-horn, twisted while standing in the stirrups to look back, then eased back down as he rubbed a hand over his scratchy face and said, "Can we approach the soddy without being seen?"

She shook her head. "No. That's why it's out in the middle of open country. They're not fools, Ashe. Well, the ones that run things aren't." She looked up ahead. "We can wait until dusk if you're dead set on goin' up there. But I think it's a total waste of time. They've had plenty of time to load wagons with the presses and whatnot and head out of the country."

"Maybe we could overtake them."

She looked aghast. "The two of us? Hell, you *are* crazy, Ashe. Those wagons's will be surrounded by half the Mormon militia. We couldn't even skulk up on 'em in the darkness, but even if we could—"

"All right. All right. You don't have to preach a sermon. But we'll still go to the soddy. They sure as hell didn't sweep the place out. I need something, even if it's only incriminating scraps of paper or broken printing press parts, to prove that's where they made the damned money."

She leaned on the saddlehorn regarding him. "Answer a question for me. There are armed men ready to shoot us on sight all over the damned countryside, an' why can't you just wait until your friends start mixin' it with the others—then, after that's ended, ride to the soddy and collect your incriminatin' evidence?"

He gazed at her with resentment rising. He'd learned to respect her. He'd learned to admire her. He'd even been deferring to her judgment the last day or so. As he now told her, up until now she'd probably been his salvation, but from now on he'd do the planning.

Her reaction was not the eruption of scathing words he'd expected and was braced for. It was a slow welling of tears, as though he'd spoken words that cut into her heart more than insulted her mind.

He was nonplussed until she turned the big colt and started riding northward, keeping her back to him as she rode. Then he tried to get up there to ride stirrup with her. She'd have none of it. She'd squeeze the big colt just enough to stay a few yards ahead.

He gave it up and slouched along behind her, muttering to himself to the effect that woman and the weather shared a common virtue: Neither was completely predictable.

CHAPTER 10

The Five Faces of Death

THEY were forced to stop when broken country, tall underbrush, and scatterings of trees ended and open, semidesert
grazing country prevailed. Amilie was still having no part of
him, but he acted as though whatever he'd said back yonder
hadn't created the first crisis between them. He eyed the
coppery heavens and said, "What d'you think? Couple of
hours before dusk?"

She didn't answer. She was sitting her saddle, staring
straight ahead, both hands atop the saddlehorn. He felt like
sighing. Then he felt like swearing. But he did neither
because both their mounts threw up their heads at the same
time, ears pointing slightly to the east.

This time the sighting of riders left Colby with no doubts.
For one thing, they were coming from the wrong direction
to be the men he knew were somewhere to the west. Another
thing was that they rode as men did who were thoroughly
familiar with the terrain. He eased around and told Amilie
to do the same.

When they'd been safely concealed by underbrush behind
a jumble of light gray, huge rocks where they dismounted,
she spoke, but did not look at him as she did so. "They're
headin' for the ranch."

He stared at her. "The old man and his boys?"

"Maybe, but it looked like more than three riders to me."

After answering him she turned slowly to look behind
them, down their back trail. "By now those five manhunters
have found Jack and Don." With a hint of spite in her voice

75

she said, "What was it you told me about fugitives havin' to keep moving? We wasted a lot of time back there with Jack an' Don, an' we're addin' to it right now."

He stepped away from their concealment to find those oncoming riders. He saw their dust long before he saw them, and for a fact they did appear to be heading for the Rigdon place. But of one thing he was fairly certain, the Rigdons were not among them. As he turned back he told himself she was right; the country was filling up with riders. He'd kicked a hornet's nest sure enough.

When he returned, she looked stonily at him as she said, "Well?"

"There's five of them. It's not the Rigdons."

"Of course not. By now they're well on the way up to St. George with the wagons and their armed outriders. You didn't get to know old Sidney very well, after all. He never, since I was small, ever rode into trouble if there was a way to ride around it."

Colby reached inside his shirt to scratch. "Behind us, ahead of us, all around us."

She showed him an icy smile and said, "You're the Arizona Ranger. You give the orders. I'm just a female. Which way from here?"

Exasperated, he tried to make amends by saying, "Amilie, what I said was that from now on I'd—"

"I know what you said an' why you said it. Hell, everything was fine as long as you needed me to get you away from the pursuit, because I knew the country, but now—"

"*Stop it!*"

She flinched but did not drop her eyes.

He hung fire before proceeding. "Sure, I needed you. I still need you. Amilie, it's got to be a habit, needin' you. What I didn't get across very well was that, sure, you know the land, but I got experience in the kind of a mess we're in. I never meant to—"

"Ashe, just tell me one thing: Why is it that men can't abide the notion of a woman bein' a partner with them?"

He raised his hat, wiped sweat with a soiled sleeve, and lowered the hat. It was hot. What shade the concealing underbrush offered was thin and meager. "They *can* abide it. Just think back. The more you took the lead, the more you got to makin' all the decisions too, like I was a wet-pants kid."

"I did no such a thing!"

"You did!"

Her gaze faltered for the first time. She made a pained little forced grin at him. "I didn't know I was doin' it. I didn't mean to. Are you sure?"

"Sure as shootin' I'm sure." He met her strange little smile with a soft grin and offered her his right hand. "Partners. Equal partners. I'll listen to you an' you listen to me."

She held his hand in a surprisingly powerful grip. As their eyes met and held, Colby felt as though his breath was without adequate oxygen. At least his heart came to a slow, steady, rough beat, the way it had other times in his life when he'd been in high-altitude country.

Her color seemed to be receding. Neither of them released the hand of the other one. He had a sudden flash of insight; her tears back yonder, her hostility afterward right up until this moment.

Good gawd, she was a woman!

She said, "Your palm's sweaty."

He released her hand. He had to say something, anything. "I'd sure like a bath an' a shave."

She snickered. "You could use both. . . . Ashe?"

"What?"

"Do you like me?"

He eyed the lowering far sun when he replied. "Yes, I like you. Amilie, you got any idea how old I am?"

Her answer was a long time coming, and when the words

finally arrived, they sounded like rocks striking glass. "Behind us. Hear them coming?"

The drowsing horses had heard them earlier and were peering southward. That was all Colby and Amilie needed. They got astride, and as she took the lead, she said, "There's not a hell of a lot we can do but sashay around until dark." As she led him down alongside the dark vertical rise of a crumbly barranca, she also said, "Maybe we should head for the ranch. They wouldn't expect us to be up there, would they? And we could lose our tracks in all the other tracks out there. What do you think?"

Despite their peril, he smiled to himself: she was deferring to him out of politeness because her own mind was made up.

"Amilie . . . have you ever been kissed?"

Her back stiffened from hips to shoulder as she rode ahead of him. When she eventually spoke again, they were leaving the concealment of the sandstone barranca, heading into boulder country where bunchgrass grew in tall profusion and thornpin, catclaw, and other antisocial plants flourished, some taller than a mounted man.

"Once. Sam'l grabbed me in the barn. It was awful. He smelled, he hadn't shaved. I hit him but he's strong."

"What happened?"

"Mrs. Rigdon heard me swearing and squawking in the barn. She was next door gatherin' eggs in the henhouse. She came into the barn like a bear, hit Sam'l over the head with her egg basket, and if I hadn't been so scairt I'd have dropped down laughin' at him standing there with egg dripping over him and his mother hittin' him hard every time she swung until he threw up his arms and ran."

Colby had another question, when up ahead Amilie's big colt faltered, then stopped of its own accord. He heard the girl's breath whistle out. He could see nothing until he reined up beside her.

Maybe it was inevitable, maybe it wasn't; maybe it was just bad luck, but there were five mounted men sitting across their path. Large, bearded men, whose faces were shaded by broad-brimmed hats. Their carbines were slung under their saddle fenders, six-guns at their waists, hands resting atop saddlehorns as the men stared expressionlessly at Colby and Amilie.

Unlike Don and Jack back there, these strangers were older, grizzled, sagacious, and as grim-faced as death itself. Colby had never seen any of them before.

In the back of his mind a fierce thought arrived: *You damned fool! Ten years manhunting and you pushed your luck when a ten-year-old would've known the odds were much too great! You were thinking about the girl and now by gawd you're going to pay for it. They will kill you—and her too!*

The nearest of the large, roughly dressed men had streaks of gray in his beard and narrowed, ice-blue eyes. He turned aside to expectorate amber, straightened around, and said, "Get rid of the guns."

Colby and Amilie obeyed.

The big man sat, as imposing as a massive statue, looking steadily at them as though he had all the time in the world. And for his purpose, he probably did.

When he spoke next, he ignored Colby. "You know who I am, girl?"

She knew. "Yes. When I've delivered the bundles you were there."

The man spat again, resettled his cud in the opposite cheek, and glanced at his silent, watching companions. "Rigdon's girl."

Colby concluded the four men sitting there did not know Amilie, at least not by sight. If these were the same five riders they'd seen earlier, then something had turned them off their approach to the ranch. If they weren't the same five, then how had they known to be sitting there waiting?

The spokesman shifted the gaze of his pale eyes to Colby. "The law!" he exclaimed. "You don't look like the law. You look like a run-down, unwashed wildhorseman or a cowboy. Your name's Colby?"

Colby nodded. There was no point in denying anything, because when they got around to it, they'd search him.

"Well now, Mister Colby, my name's Porter Hanson. I want you to tell us how you come to be up here, how you got up here, and who-all's up here with you, an' about the only thing I can think of that'll keep you alive is the truth." Porter Hanson paused to consider his friends, the nearest of whom had an ivory-handled six-gun with six file marks just below the hammer on a little, rounded steel housing. Hanson said, "This here is my associate, Mister McKenna." Hanson faced Colby again, still unruffled and unhurried. "He's from up at St. George an' he's heard some interestin' stories up there. Now then, you tell us what we want to know an' if it don't jibe with what Mister McKenna knows, you spend eternity right here."

Colby's shock had passed. He risked asking a question of Porter Hanson. "How did you know where to intercept us?"

Hanson's pale eyes showed bleak amusement as he replied. "Well now, that steel mirror you hung in a tree up yonder, it was Mister McKenna's idea to have a man get on a higher barranca to the east an', as soon as he seen two riders, to flash his mirror. One long flash if you was comin' north. Two if you was goin' west, an' three if you was headin' east. Mister Colby, you didn't see no flashes because we was up north on our way to the ranch. He flashed his signal northward, not southward where you'd have seen it. Does that answer you?"

Before Colby could speak, the hawk-faced man with the ivory-stocked six-gun snarled. "My horse is thirsty an' this is just one of 'em, Porter. Let's get it over with."

As he was speaking, McKenna drew the six-gun and held it uncocked in his lap while awaiting Hanson's reply.

Hanson leaned to dismount. "Put everythin' you got in your hat, Mister Colby, then dismount. Girl, you—"

She spat at him like a cougar. "You damned old outlaw! They're goin' to surround every last one of you!"

Hanson was on the ground beside his big horse when he asked who was going to surround them, and that set Amilie off again. As Colby listened to her, he groaned inwardly.

"The Arizona Rangers, that's who!"

Hanson smiled to show chewing-tobacco-stained big teeth. "Young lady, there's four of 'em takin' their time comin' down from St. George, pretendin' to be range riders. An' behind them four gents is six of our men, but even if there warn't, no four Rangers could surround us."

Colby held his breath, expecting Amilie's anger to make her blurt out that there was another, larger group of Rangers approaching from the west.

She mentioned something altogether different. "They'll catch your wagons headin' for St. George."

That statement held each of the five old men perfectly still as they stared. McKenna's voice was soft as silk when he spoke. "Who told you there was any wagons?"

She put her defiant stare on him when she said, "Sid Rigdon."

Even Colby was stopped dead in his tracks by that lie. McKenna and the other men, still sitting their saddles, shot a quick look at Porter Hanson. He was regarding Amilie with a piercing stare. "You're lying," he told her, but one of the other men, a barrel-built individual with a bull neck, was not convinced of this. "Then how in hell would she have known about the wagons?" he demanded of Hanson.

Hanson had no ready answer for that. He could not have guessed the truth at this time, although later he or someone might have. Whoever came across those two bound men back yonder. Don and Jack.

When Hanson did not answer, another of his companions growled at him. "Port, remember what Brig told us last summer? He said he didn't completely trust Rigdon."

Hanson relaxed his stance with reins dangling from one big hand.

McKenna brought the subject back where he wanted it. "Damn it all, let's get this over with an' get to riding." He raised the ivory-gripped six-gun and was about to swing it to bear on Colby when another man growled at him.

"Wait a minute. I don't like this."

McKenna turned on him. "What don't you like? You knew when we started the hunt what we'd do when we—"

"Not that," the other man said sharply. "I don't care about that. What I don't like is that if old Rigdon shot off his mouth to her, who else did he shoot it off to, an' just what the hell is he really up to? Tryin' to save his bacon by maybe playin' both sides? I've heard enough about the old bastard to believe he'd do it if he was hard pressed. You shoot them two, Mister McKenna, an' if this don't come out right, if they do catch us . . . I got to tell you I could make out with a few years in prison, but not gettin' hanged for no damned murder. *That's* what I don't like!"

McKenna glared at the speaker, but the bullnecked man cut across his forming words. "Jethro's right," he told McKenna before switching his attention to Porter Hanson.

"I don't think no Rangers is goin' to catch us, but it wouldn't hurt to have these two along in case we need somethin' to use as a trade-off. Porter, we been settin' here half a damned hour. For all we know, the others are already leaving the country. I say let's head north an' take these two with us."

For the first time since this argument had erupted Hanson seemed in agreement with something that had been said. He gestured toward two of his companions as he swung back into the saddle. "You lads take their reins. Let's go."

CHAPTER 11

Through the Night

ONE rider, the bullnecked man, turned back to seek the manhunters who had been tracking the fugitives. He would tell them of the capture and no doubt of everything else, including what Amilie had said about Sidney Rigdon.

Colby hadn't had to empty his pockets after all, nor did his four bearded companions pay as much attention to him and Amilie as they did to hushed discussions among themselves. As Colby watched, he could have hugged the girl. Whether she'd thought her lie through or had just uttered it off the top of her head, the effect was the same: their captors were upset.

They should have turned west a mile or so on their way. The Rigdon place was over there, but they did not even look west, much less rein in that direction.

Porter Hanson dropped back to ride with the prisoners as another man split off in a loose lope heading west. Evidently part of the mutterings that neither Colby nor Amilie could hear had to do with putting a scout out. What bothered Colby was that a lone horseman riding west could be mistaken for Colby himself, in which case he and Amilie might get shot when the scout raced back. *If* he raced back.

As Porter reined in beside Colby, the older man said, "How'd you get up here?"

There was nothing to be gained by being sly about it, so Colby told him. Hanson rode a fair distance, mulling that over before he said, "A man's got to be awful lucky to come up through the reservation this time of year. Any time, for that matter."

Colby could have agreed with him but he didn't.

Hanson continued to slouch along beside Colby. He eventually spoke again. "You'n Sidney got along all right, did you?"

Colby nodded. "Yep. Have you talked to him since I escaped?"

"Out at the—out near an old soddy I did, but everyone was in a hurry so we didn't get to talk much. He did say how he ambushed you and the girl helped him do it. Mister Colby, just why'n hell did you burden yourself with a woman? You could've traveled a lot faster'n farther without her."

"She knows the country; I don't." Colby watched the older man gnaw on a lint-encrusted plug and get a ragged chunk of molasses-cured inside his mouth. "Are we goin' all the way up to St. George?" Colby asked.

Hanson nodded his head while leaning to spray juice at a running lizard. He scored a direct hit; the lizard faltered, then reversed itself and ran right into the way of the horses. They ignored him. He had a narrow squeak but emerged, doubling back in his own tracks, slightly smaller than he had been; a horse had unknowingly stepped on his tail. He jettisoned it and was now nearly completely tailless as he dove into the first thicket available.

There were now three captors. One was that garrulous individual someone had called Jethro, another was McKenna with his elegant six-gun. The third man was Porter Hanson. But if there had been only one man, Colby would still not have risked being cut in two by someone with a gun as he made an unarmed attack.

McKenna hadn't said much since they'd ridden away from the capture site. It was Colby's opinion that while the others might have some qualms about murdering two prisoners, McKenna would have none at all.

Porter Hanson yanked Colby's thought back to the present with a question. "From what I've heard, Arizona Rangers got some good men, so maybe you can tell me why they'd be ignorant enough to send your four friends up here and not give us credit for havin' the brains to figure out who they was?"

Colby was groping when Amilie on his far side offered a smooth reply. "That's exactly what they figured; ignorant folks in a starve-out country couldn't be too smart or they wouldn't live down here."

Hanson squinted. "Is that what Colby told you, girl?"

"Yes," Amilie retorted with no hesitation, unwilling to meet the look she was getting from Ashe Colby.

Hanson rode squinting up ahead where daylight was beginning to get its late-day cast. The man called Jethro looked around and grinned. "Somewhere up ahead we'd ought to meet them four Rangers and the lads from St. George who'll be shaggin' 'em." Jethro thought briefly, then added a little more. "An' maybe overtake the wagons."

No one offered either denial or confirmation, leaving Colby with the impression that Jethro was not taken very seriously by his companions.

Porter Hanson appeared lost in thought, but eventually he leaned to see around Colby and addressed the girl. "Sidney been holdin' out, has he?"

She knit her brow when she answered. "How would I know? All they ever told me was to deliver the bundles. Once, I rode out there with 'em, to the soddy I mean, but they wouldn't let me see inside."

That seemed to satisfy Hanson, because he eased back in the saddle and looked up ahead where McKenna had just discovered wagon tracks and was pointing to them. Hanson nodded without comment.

Colby saw the tracks, but they interested him less than approaching nightfall. When darkness arrived, the Rangers coming in from the west would be unable to see fresh tracks going north; nor was he convinced that when they eventually did see them, they'd turn northward. Their purpose in being in this territory was to find the place where counterfeit money was manufactured, to hunt Colby down for whatever information he'd ferreted out, then to move through the area making arrests. There was no reason to think any of them would know Colby had been captured and was now being taken to a town far from the Wolf Hole area.

McKenna jarred everyone out of their reveries when he said, "I thought I heard wagons."

Hanson called a halt and everyone strained for recognizable sounds. McKenna was right. But although the sounds grew louder as they resumed their ride, increasing the gait a little, they did not actually see the wagons. Dusk came quickly and just as quickly became night.

Colby frowned to himself. By his estimate those wagons should have been miles farther ahead. He arrived at a logical reason why they weren't by guessing that loaded as they were with printing presses, made mostly of cast iron, they couldn't make very good time even though the ground was hard enough to support them. Two draft animals to each wagon, with ninety miles of pulling ahead of them, could not be hurried unless the teamsters wanted to end up with horses so worked-down they couldn't move at all.

Jethro was out front by about fifteen yards. He was ignoring the riders behind him and concentrating on the groans, grinds, and creaking sounds of the wagons when Colby felt a cool hand brush him on the off side. He looked around as Amilie pressed something cold and unyielding into his hand. It was her little gambler model revolver.

He rode looking straight ahead with the weapon nearly hidden by his hand, which he pressed against a trouser leg. If Porter Hanson turned his head while Colby was trying to sneak the weapon inside his shirt, Hanson might be content to simply disarm him, but that hawk-faced, bleak man up ahead with the ivory-handled Colt could be relied upon to react differently.

Colby was sweating like a stud-horse and it was no longer hot. It was warm but getting less so by the minute. He inched the hand up against his body until he could feel for a gap in his shirtfront, then he waited until Hanson had looped his reins and was concentrating on slicing off a fresh cud before very stealthily pushing the weapon inside his shirt and into the top of his britches where it felt cold. Where it also felt very uncomfortable as his horse hiked along.

He glared at Amilie. She smiled back very sweetly.

The event which interrupted an otherwise uneventful ride through rough country full of night-enhanced shadows was an unmistakable rattle of loping horses coming from the south. McKenna's reaction was to haul sharply around, hawk-like features menacing, right hand lightly atop the ivory-handled Colt.

Jethro turned back at a dead walk. Hanson snapped at the captives, "Not a sound." He listened until he seemed satisfied the oncoming riders were indeed riding directly toward him, then he swung to the ground, ordered everyone else to do likewise, and led his animal toward the nearest stand of underbrush.

If it had been daylight, Hanson's ruse would not have worked, but not even an Indian could read sign in the night. If there had been a full moon, it might have been possible, but there was neither a full moon nor sufficient starlight to make tracking an option. Suddenly, a band of horsemen swept past, visible only as phantoms.

When they had passed, Jethro smiled broadly, but neither McKenna nor Hanson did. McKenna grunted sourly to the effect that whoever they were, if they were other manhunters seeking Colby and the girl, when they eventually overtook the wagons they would either continue northward as an added armed escort or, if they were not friends, there would probably be a fight up ahead.

Hanson grunted as he toed into the stirrup without commenting. He glanced at Colby and jerked his head for the prisoners to follow his example.

This time, as they struck out, Hanson growled at Jethro to continue scouting ahead but to be very careful and not get too far ahead.

He might as well have been speaking to a tree; Jethro struck out still grinning and was shortly lost to sight. Hanson wagged his head, but when McKenna threatened to go after Jethro, Hanson growled at him: "You stay back."

McKenna rode on the far side of Amilie while Colby was between the girl and Porter Hanson.

Their new course was still northward, but on an easterly angle. None of them tried to get a conversation going; each of them was concentrating on what might eventually occur far ahead when those riders overtook the wagons.

Colby was able to reach inside and get the little pistol shoved around until it no longer gouged him. He did this by pretending to be scratching, but neither Hanson nor McKenna paid him the slightest attention. They were waiting for an eruption over where the wagons were rolling. The more time passed, the more Hanson relaxed, probably convinced that those phantom horsemen had been friends. But McKenna didn't loosen at all, and when Amilie said something pleasant to him, he snarled her into silence.

Colby had something on his mind besides those riders and the wagons. Sooner or later they were going to have to stop and rest the animals. Whether this would happen near water or not, he had no idea because he had never before been in this northward country, but when it happened he would have a clear choice of either trying to reverse his situation by using the little pistol, or deciding to wait for something to occur which might increase his chances of success.

One thing was damned clear: the moment he pointed that little gun he might make Hanson hesitate, but not McKenna. So he speculated about trying to get very close to McKenna, preferably directly behind him at about arm's distance, before cocking the pistol. Even then it would be almighty risky. Colby had met a number of men like McKenna in his time, and as he'd been told from the beginning of his lawman's career, when a man was certain an adversary would react violently, shoot first and keep right on shooting until you were sure he was stone dead.

He glanced at Amilie, expecting her to be drooping in the saddle. They'd been many hours without sleep or decent food. She was riding straight up in the saddle and met his gaze with a mischievous smile, then leaned to pat the neck of her big roan colt.

Colby rolled and lit a smoke. McKenna, who had not once since the capture even offered a less than threatening look, leaned back and said, "Can you spare a little of that?"

Colby passed over the sack and papers. McKenna rolled a cigarette, lit it inside his hat to minimize the abrupt brilliance, handed back the makings, and unbent just enough to nod curtly and say, "Thanks."

Whoever McKenna's parents had been, they had at least started him out right. Whatever else he had become by middle life, he had retained at least some of the earlier amenities that had been drilled into him.

Porter Hanson broke the long silence. "One of us better scout up the ruins," he said, and without answering, McKenna urged his horse ahead in a slow lope, riding more eastward than northward.

Hanson saw Colby's quizzical expression and explained. "There's some old mud houses up here around a blue-water spring. As far as I know, it's the only water until we cross the line up into Utah." Indifferently, Hanson added a little more. "One of them old-time Indian villages where they built one room above the other ones. What Mexicans call a pueblo."

It was an accurate description as far as it went, but when they met McKenna at the outskirts of the place, what deluges had not damaged, earthquakes and the simple passage of time had. What Colby recognized as one of those prehistoric Indian pueblos was now largely eroded mounds of ancient adobe.

Colby said to Amilie, "Now *this* place is haunted," meaning that the canyon they'd ridden through and which she'd said was haunted was not—at least not in the way this ancient abandoned village was.

They dismounted, loosened cinchas, removed bridles, and stood hipshot as their animals tanked up. Afterward, Colby and Amilie followed McKenna to a massively walled cube of a house with one door and one square window-hole to rest.

Then, without any warning, all hell broke loose up ahead somewhere, and westerly. For five seconds no one said a word, then McKenna exploded with profanity and glared at Hanson. "They're attackin' the wagons!"

Hanson stood, head cocked, looking in the direction of the gunfire. His reaction undoubtedly enraged McKenna, but to Colby it was consistent with Hanson's temperament. Without any hint of outrage, he said, "Sure sounds like it. And what can we do about it? Nothing."

McKenna hauled up as stiff as a ramrod. "Get rid of these two and get over there. They need help."

McKenna's last three words were correct. Distant gunfire did not dwindle to intermittent firing for a long time. The fight sounded like a pitched battle, although in the dark of night anyone's shooting accuracy would be questionable, so men threw a lot of lead in the hope of occasionally inflicting casualties.

Hanson listened a moment, then replied to McKenna. "By the time we could get over there, Mac, there won't be no need." He and the angry man faced each other, McKenna straining to get into the fight, Hanson just as resolved not to. Finally, Hanson gestured and said, "Go, if you want to, an' when you find Jethro send him back here."

McKenna did not reply, he was gauging the rattle of gunfire; it was just now beginning to become less thunderous, a little more intermittent, as though the first surprise attack was over and now the grim business of sniping had begun.

He threw down his two rolled blankets, would not look at any of them, and stood in the low doorway looking out into the night and listening. Behind him, Hanson, Colby, and Amilie used their meager resources to prepare for a rest.

One thing all four of them, captives and captors, could have agreed upon—and which none of them mentioned—was that those men who had attacked the wagons were not friends nor accomplices of the men with the wagons; that had significance for all four of them.

CHAPTER 12

"She'll Do It!"

IT was impossible to relax as long as that distant fight was audibly in progress, so Colby chewed jerky beside Amilie, and when Hanson joined McKenna in the doorway Colby leaned to whisper. "If they knew you kept that little gun, they'd skin you alive."

Instead of replying, she jutted her chin toward where their two captors were muttering with their backs to the seated prisoners. Her meaning was obvious.

Colby considered their chances and whispered his reply to her mute suggestion. "Not yet. I'll do it when the time is right."

She scowled at him in obvious disapproval but said nothing.

McKenna needed another smoke and turned back into the room while Hanson walked out into the night, probably to care for the animals. McKenna hunkered down and worked up a smoke from Colby's makings. After lighting up he regarded the prisoners stonily. "Colby, or whatever your name is, if that's them four Rangers who come up the road pretendin' to be riders lookin' for work, this here is their last fight. There's more'n four outriders with the wagons, an' there's two men with each wagon." McKenna's lips pulled back from his teeth. "An' there's men from St. George trailin' your friends from up yonder."

The gunfire abruptly ended. Colby and Amilie waited for it to resume, but it never did, and McKenna's wolfish smile broadened. "That's how long it takes us fellers to put down Arizona Rangers."

Against his better judgment Colby successfully planted a doubt in McKenna's mind by saying, "How would those four Rangers know about the wagons coming up here from down yonder?"

McKenna's eyes slowly lost their triumphant gleam in the semidarkness. He took a long pull off the cigarette and exhaled just as slowly. "Maybe you signaled them," he snarled, but the improbability of this made it seem unlikely even to the man who made the statement. He got up and left the gloomy, stale-scented room in search of Hanson.

That gave Amilie a chance to speak aloud, but very softly. "If you'd had the gun in your hand just now . . . hell, he wasn't more'n ten feet from you."

He peered at her as though doubting that he'd heard her correctly. "How could I have had that gun in my hand? Even if I'd had it, Amilie, one shot—whether it downed McKenna or not—would stir Hanson up." He frowned at her. "Wait. Just wait."

She may have been impressed with his logic, but whether she was or not the next thing she said was on an altogether different subject. "Could that have been your friends attackin' the wagons?"

"Maybe. They're sure as hell out here by now. If they caught Jethro or any of the others and got the truth out of them . . . it damned well could be."

"In which case . . . ?"

"In which case we do exactly as we been doing. We keep out of trouble with Hanson and McKenna, and wait."

A few minutes later McKenna returned alone. He sank down near his blanket roll beside the only doorway and got comfortable against the massive mud wall at his back as he said, "Hanson's rode over to see what he can smell out. You two can stretch out if you want to. First, toss me the tobacco sack an' papers."

Colby tossed them over. Amilie addressed the gunman in her sweet tone of voice. It had a different effect upon McKenna than it had had on Ashe Colby, who, over the past few days, had learned one particular thing about Amilie: when she used that sweet-as-honey tone, watch out! She said, "What's the purpose in takin' us all the way to St. George?"

McKenna's reply was direct and factual. "Because no one from Arizona with a badge has any authority in Utah, an' the folks up there are just as cranky about that as the Mexicans are when U.S. lawmen try to sneak over the line and arrest outlaws down in their country."

Amilie looked at Colby, who just barely inclined his head in agreement with McKenna.

She continued, using the same sweet tone. "If that's Rangers over there who attacked the wagons, an' if they came out on top, an' if they didn't kill Sidney Rigdon, I'll tell you how he'll get away."

McKenna blew smoke in Amilie's direction when he said, "How?"

"Trade them the money box."

She deliberately let those four words hang between them until McKenna straightened up off the wall and looked steadily through the semigloom at her. "What money box?"

"The one he's got hid at the ranch. The one his wife told me he keeps eight thousand dollars in. Eight thousand in good money. Not counterfeit. She was tellin' me how sly he was. She said that money's to buy himself out of trouble if he ever has to."

McKenna's cigarette went out between his lips as he stared at the girl. He glanced once at Colby then back to the girl. He got to his feet, leaned in the doorway for a long time, then turned back and snarled. "Lie belly-down an' put your hands behind you."

Colby got just one opportunity to meet Amilie's gaze before he had to obey McKenna. If looks could have killed, there would have been no reason for McKenna to tie Amilie. She would have been as shriveled as a mummy.

As the gunman was lashing their ankles and wrists, Amilie spoke to him one more time. "For tellin' you Mister Rigdon's secret, you owe me."

McKenna said nothing. He yanked their bonds tight and knotted them. As he was arising, Amilie spoke again. "The least you could do is give us a chance to run for it before Mister Hanson gets back."

McKenna swore and stamped out of the room. As Colby was about to speak, Amilie hissed him into silence. Not until they heard a horse leaving in a rush did she smile at her bound companion as she said, "She did tell me her husband had a cache, but she didn't say how much money was in it."

He was too dumbfounded to speak for a moment. She also said, "McKenna didn't ride northwest. Did you listen for that? He's not goin' over where the fight was an' try to find old Sidney. He circled around this place and went straight south."

Colby relaxed against the hard earthen floor, gazing into the gloom at the low mud ceiling. He did not know what to say. He could have sworn at her; that's what he felt like doing. Instead he lay in silence so long she scooted over, rolled onto her side, and said, "Use your teeth and untie my hands. Ashe, we don't have all night. There's still Mister Hanson an' Jethro."

He had to jackknife along the floor to get close enough to go to work on the wrist bindings. He stopped once to listen, then to say, "Someday you're goin' to get yourself killed, an' anyone who's with you."

Her reply was flat and forthright. "Not if I have to wait for you to do something, I won't."

He worked as best he could and was beginning to feel thoroughly exasperated when she spoke again. "Someone's coming."

He rolled away and pushed up into a sitting position. He heard nothing. She said, "Put your ear against the ground."

He ignored that to drop back down and renew his gnawing and wrenching until he felt the bonds loosen, then he jack-knifed back into a sitting position facing the door as he said, "Pull. Your hands'll come out."

About the time she stopped straining and grunting, they both heard a shod horse enter the ancient village from the northwest. Colby said to her, "It's Hanson. Keep your hands behind you."

She twisted to reach behind his back, but he jerked away. "Leave me be. There's not enough time. Sit up an' act like you're still tied."

He was right. Hanson's approaching footsteps were notice-able by the ring of his spurs right up until he stepped into the doorway with a gun in his fist. He looked at them, around the room, leathered the Colt, and said, "Where's McKenna?"

Colby said, "Gone. About fifteen minutes ago."

Hanson walked in and stood looking down at them. "Why? What happened?"

Amilie's voice sounded perfectly natural when she said, "He thought whoever attacked the wagons had won. He said more'n likely they was lawmen an' he wasn't goin' to stay here an' be caught in this little room with only one door when they come chargin' over here."

The big man stood a moment in thought, and even if it hadn't been too gloomy in the room to see his face and read the expression there, his full beard would have concealed the expression anyway.

He returned to the doorway, and while he seemed to be testing the night for sounds, Amilie reached over, plunged a hand inside Colby's shirt, groped until she found the little gun, and yanked her hand away. Colby could do nothing but glare as she put both her hands behind her back and ignored his look. She did not take her eyes off Hanson's back until he started to turn. Then she lowered her eyes, and in the poor light her expression was either demure or demoralized, but certainly Hanson had no reason to consider her a threat. He moved a little closer along the front wall, blew out a big breath, and leaned over there as he groped for his plug; he used both hands, one to hold it and the other to begin to skive off a cud with his knife. That's when Amilie moved . . . and Colby held his breath.

Hanson wouldn't scare easily, and even if she shot him with that little gun, unless she hit a vital spot, he would still be able to kill them both with his big-bored six-gun. Colby was no coward, but he knew a lot about guns and killing. He wouldn't have done what Amilie was doing, which was the main reason he was still alive after ten years of going up against killers.

She did not move fast as she brought both hands around in front and aimed the little gun. She was cocking it when Hanson opened his mouth to take the cud, his knife-hand high, his other hand holding the plug of chewing tobacco.

Nobody made a sound. Porter Hanson stared as though he could not believe what he saw. He was still holding the knife poised with the tobacco on it when Amilie said, "Drop the plug. *Drop it!*"

As Hanson's fingers opened and the plug fell, she said, "Reach with that hand, the left one. Use just your fingers an' lift out that gun and drop it too. Mister Hanson, don't ever forget that a woman will kill faster'n a man will. *Shuck the gun!*"

Hanson moved as slowly as a sleepwalker would have. When his Colt fell, Amilie said, "Lie belly-down with your arms pushed far out in front. Are you deaf? *I'll kill you!*"

Hanson was still holding the cud poised on the side of his knife. Colby could tell Hanson had recovered from his astonishment, because he put the tobacco into his mouth, snapped the knife closed, and lowered his hand. Colby put in his two bits' worth. "She can't miss at that distance."

Hanson worked the cud into place with his tongue, spat,

and lowered his head slightly. "She won't shoot," he told Colby. "She's a woman."

Colby snorted a bitter, little laugh. "Mister Hanson, I've seen her use a gun. You're goin' to get yourself killed if you don't get down."

Hanson went down to his knees, glared, then got all the way down and shoved both arms out ahead. Amilie jumped up, waited until Colby had freed her ankles, and walked over behind Porter Hanson; she leaned to place the cold snout of her little gun at the base of his skull in back, then picked up his six-gun and tossed it toward Colby. She pulled loose the big man's belt, yanked it as hard as she could around his ankles, left him like that, head slightly off the ground watching. She returned to free Colby and waited until he was upright with Hanson's gun in his fist before returning to use Hanson's bandana to lash his wrists in back. As she was arising, she toed him over onto his back, aimed squarely between his eyes, and stood there with both men scarcely breathing.

She eased down the hammer, let the little gun hang at her side, and looked back where Colby was standing like a statue. "Let's go. Should we take him back with us or leave him here?"

Colby said nothing until he'd removed Hanson's shell-belt and buckled it around his own middle so he'd have something to hold the six-gun. Then he looked at Amilie. The little gambler's pistol was shoved into the front of her britches. She smiled at him. "If we haul him along he's goin' to be a burden."

Colby nodded, stepped away toward the door, and as Amilie preceded him out into the chilly late night he looked down. Hanson was looking straight at him. Colby wagged his head. "She would have done it," he said, and followed Amilie out where the horses had been picking scant growths of pale grass.

As they rigged out and got astride, Amilie said nothing.

Even after they were picking their way back southward she was quiet. Colby knew she was watching him but ignored that until they'd covered several miles, then he turned, caught her gazing at him, and said, "I meant it, Amilie. Someday you're goin' to get yourself killed."

Her answer was straightforward. "Something had to be done. If they got us all the way up to St. George, the folks up there would have locked us up and flung the key away. Colby, you don't know these people. They're opinionated, stubborn, and as unforgiving as stone."

It was true he did not know the people, at least not as well as she obviously did, but he knew how people got killed. He rode again in silence for a while before speaking to her again. "I want your promise you won't pull a gun again unless I tell you to."

Her answer came swiftly and without an argument. "All right. You have my word."

He eyed her skeptically but kept his thoughts to himself as they headed back southward in the direction of the Rigdon place.

CHAPTER 13

Toward Dawn

THEY halted out a fair distance. The sky was beginning to softly brighten and it was cold. Dawn was coming as they sat like a pair of broncos looking in the direction of the Rigdon buildings. There were no lights; even at that distance the yard was ghostly quiet, empty-seeming. To Amilie, who had spent most of her life there, the place had a frighteningly haunted feel.

She did not believe they should go down there. "Why are we here, Ashe? What if McKenna's still here looking for that money?"

"I don't see any sign of him," he said shortly. "I'll be careful going in, but we've got to have fresh horses. We've given these animals about all they can handle."

"There won't be any horses."

He wasn't convinced of that or he wouldn't have come here. "You stay out here. I'll slip around behind the barn before daylight and see." As he was swinging to the ground he also said, "We've got to have 'em. If we can't get 'em here, we got to find 'em somewhere else, but we got to have fresh animals." He handed her his reins, saw the look on her face, and gave her arm a reassuring squeeze before turning away to trot in a westerly direction so he would be able to keep the barn between himself and the house.

She swung to the ground, moved to the head of the horses, and squatted. She was not aware of the chill, but she was very much aware of an uncomfortable premonition she had, which seemed to be coming out to her from the dark, broodingly silent old buildings.

An odd thing happened. A little red fox, approaching from the west in a quick trot without pausing as foxes usually did, moved directly eastward not fifty feet from where Amilie was hunkering down. When the handsome little animal was in front of Amilie, it stopped, looked directly at her for a moment, then continued on its eastward way. It did not leap out in a belly-down desperate rush the way wild animals normally did when suddenly confronted by a human being, it did not increase its gait at all as it trotted off into the sooty predawn and disappeared.

Amilie shuddered. It was cold, but that's not why she shuddered.

There was no sign of Colby. She knew he could take care of himself under most circumstances, but no one could do much about the kind of mystical danger she sensed.

Colby was coming in from the west toward the rear barn opening when a barn owl soared on silent wings above his head. The nocturnal hunter was heading for the perch where he'd spend the daylight hours. Colby stopped to watch. The bird made a graceful downward swoop at the rear of the barn, then sailed through the opening as he pumped both wings for altitude. His perch was evidently somewhere among the pole rafters.

Colby waited. If the bird returned in full flight, it would signify something was inside the barn that was not usually in there.

The bird did not fly back out. Colby resumed his stalk, got up against the rough exterior of the barn, and hung there listening and looking.

It was quiet enough to hear a mouse scampering. Colby heard nothing and began to doubt that the stalled horses the Rigdons always kept there were inside. But experience told him that horses not only sleep standing up but sleep soundest during the hours before dawn.

He eased around the opening, peeking into the kind of darkness that lingers inside windowless buildings even with the approach of dawn, took three long steps around the opening, and flattened against the wall again. He waited for his eyes to adjust to the gloom while allowing his right hand to rest upon the butt of the weapon he'd taken from Hanson.

Something rattled a stall door on its hangers. A horse moved to the upper opening of its stall and looked sleepily at Colby in the back of the barn.

Colby let his breath out silently and slowly. There was at least one horse. If there were no others, he'd take that one. He shifted slightly in order to be able to look up both lines of stalls. He thought he'd heard something near the front of the barn, so he felt along the ground for a pebble and tossed it forward.

The second horse was in the first stall on the north side near the front doorway. When it looked out for the cause of that little pebble rattling against wood, Colby saw it.

He also saw a third horse. It was easier to make out in the darkness because it was a dapple gray with a lighter-colored head. Another horse, a bay, poked his head out to also look around.

Colby stood for a long time, watching and waiting. He did not have the same premonition Amilie had, but he sensed something. It was more like a whisper in the back of his mind than a real warning.

He knew where the Rigdons kept their lead-shanks hanging, and when he felt reasonably certain it was safe to move, he went over there. The ropes with harness snaps at one end, a turk's-head knot at the other end, were hanging exactly where he'd seen them before.

Now, moving with less anxiety, he took down two shanks and was turning toward the front of the barn to catch the first animal when a very soft and quiet masculine voice said,

"That's good. You just keep one of them ropes in each hand and stand real still."

The voice was not overly menacing, but it sounded very serious. It was the voice of a man who had been lying in wait since midnight; a man who was calm, observant, and deadly—an old hand at this sort of thing.

Colby did not move. He had a fleeting thought about Amilie out there in open country with dawn coming, and speculated that if this one had been patiently waiting in the barn all night, there might possibly be at least one more of them among the other buildings also waiting, and probably watching the open country as well.

The voice seemed to have no body, at least as hard as Colby tried to see where the voice was coming from, he could not find even a faint silhouette that could have belonged to a man.

"Who are you, mister? What're you doin' here—stealing horses?"

The voice wasn't McKenna's. It sounded almost pleasant. Colby's answer was given in the same quiet manner. "Not stealing them, just trading off tired ones for fresh ones."

The voice persisted. "That don't tell me who you are."

Colby jockeyed. "Just a rider on a tired animal. Who are you?"

This time the pleasant voice was slightly harder in a flat, inflectionless way. "Get rid of the gun and walk up toward the front of the barn where I can background you."

With no choice, Colby obeyed both orders. Where he halted with a streaky kind of predawn light in the yard beyond, he turned.

Suddenly, the voice was no longer flat and threatening. "Where in the hell have you been?"

Colby didn't know how to answer that. "What do you mean?"

The voice was growing stronger, less soft and menacing. "What's your name?"

"Colby."

The voice groaned aloud. "I knew it. I was sure of it. Ashe Colby. We been lookin' for you since yesterday afternoon." The voice very abruptly acquired a physical shape as a man came up off the ground as fluidly as though he had come up out of it. He stepped ahead where he was still not entirely identifiable and holstered his weapon as he said, "Cap'n Hauser's had scouts all over hell tryin' to find you. He figured they'd caught you, so he started out accordin' to plan anyway."

The man halted in front of Colby, grinning in the gloom. "I'm Henry Knight. We met once down near Lordsburg years back."

Colby pumped the callused hand while trying to remember this man. His lack of recognition did not appear to bother Henry Knight at all. "Hell, it was six, eight years ago. There wasn't any reason for you to remember. I met you after you'n a feller named Ace Hoskins cornered those men who robbed the Las Crucas bank and handed them over to the New Mexico authorities."

From the rear of the barn a gruff voice said, "Henry, you talkin' to yourself again?"

The second man was carrying a shotgun draped from the bend of one arm as he came forward. Colby knew this one. He was the same Ace Hoskins the first man had mentioned. Hoskins's brows shot up at the sight of Colby moments before he reached with his unburdened arm to slap Colby resoundingly on the chest. "You had us scairt peeless. We caught three of 'em in an ambush east of here. Two of 'em said you'n a girl had got the drop an' left 'em tied. They said you'd most likely rode north up where the land was crawlin' with their friends. They said sure as hell you was dead by now."

Colby's tiredness descended upon him like a lead weight. "The girl's still with me. The old bastard who lived here raised her. She's out yonder with our horses waitin' for me."

Hoskins had the shotgun back in the crook of his arm as he said, "I'll go get her."

Colby shook his head. "She's got a little pistol an' she'll use it. I'll go bring her in. By the way, did you catch anyone else skulking around before I came? Who else is stakin' this place out?"

No one else had shown up, they told him. Hoskins and Knight had been left behind to guard the place while six of the other Rangers had gone upcountry to hunt for some wagons trying to get the counterfeiting equipment up over the line into Utah. They'd worked that information out of one of their captives last night.

As Colby was turning to leave the barn he said, "You fellers got anything to eat? Amilie and I haven't had a decent mouthful in a couple of days."

They looked at him. "Amilie?"

"The girl. If it wasn't for her I wouldn't be here now. Is there any grub?"

Hoskins jerked his head sideways. "The larder at the house is full of grub. I'll fire up the stove while you're bringin' her in. . . . Ashe?"

"What."

The shorter and older Ranger, the grizzled man named Henry Knight, said, "Cap'll be unhappy about you ridin' with a girl."

Colby's answer was curt. "That's too damned bad, isn't it? This one is worth three men any day of the year."

As he walked away the two Rangers exchanged a look before heading for the house. The grizzled, older one had a tart comment to make. "Since you been around Cap'n Hauser, did you ever hear him sound off on the subject of female women?"

Hoskins scowled. "No. He's got a wife, Henry."

"Wife's different, but he's got an iron rule about Rangers takin' up with women when they're working. I recall one time down near the border at a place called Piedra Negras he caught a man who was huntin' rustlers strollin' in the moonlight with as pretty a señorita as a man ever set eyes on. He fired him on the spot."

Hoskins halted at the steps to the porch. "Henry, how do you know how pretty she was?"

Knight cleared his throat before replying. "Because it was me he fired for bein' with her. Hell, I was just tryin' to get some information from her."

Ace Hoskins rolled his eyes. "That's a likely excuse. But he must have swallowed it, because you're still on the payroll."

"No, he didn't swallow it, and it was a lie anyway. But he hired me back three days later when him and me and a feller who used to ride with us named Bob Bell, who like a damned idiot went out to California to settle down, the three of us rode into an ambush and shot our way out, killed two and caught three. Cap hired me back on the spot. But this here is different. Ashe is goin' to be in trouble up to his withers."

Hoskins climbed the steps and kicked the door open as he said, "Bell? Tall, sort of scrawny feller with a peaked butt and a 'possum belly?"

Knight followed Hoskins inside where the darkness was so thick they had to approach the kitchen with their arms out as he said, "Yeah. Where'd you know him?"

"I met him a couple of times in Wagon Mound. He had a little hole-in-the-wall gunshop."

Knight watched his companion fumbling to light a lamp as he said, "That'd be him, all right. When he said he was goin' out to California, a feller asked why and Bell said to find some land, start up with some cattle, and get himself a wife." The grizzled man snorted. "He'd never get a wife. All he talked about was guns. Where's there a woman who'd put up with a man who talks about guns all the time?"

Hoskins went over to be sure the old blanket he'd hung over the only kitchen window was still in place before beginning to ransack Elizabeth Rigdon's cupboards for something to make a meal from.

He came across Rigdon's jug of popskull and placed it squarely in the center of the table, where Henry Knight eyed it owlishly before reaching for it. That was another thing Captain Hauser was dead set against: drinking when a man was supposed to be keeping a vigil.

Ace Hoskins took back the jug, slung it over his shoulder with one hand, twisted his head and drank, handed back the jug, and went to work getting the firebox of the stove stuffed with kindling. As he straightened up with the smell of burning wood beginning to fill the kitchen, he said, "I don't know. Cap's real fond of Ashe. He might not get roiled up about the woman."

His friend cocked back a chair, shoved his hat back, and watched Hoskins at the stove. "Don't bet any money on it," he said, and shot back up to his feet at the sounds coming across from the barn.

Hoskins saw this and spoke shortly. "That's them. Set down. It's daylight now. There's no one else comin' in here or they'd have been here by now. Say, that Rigdon woman must've spent every wakin' moment puttin' up food."

"If you was a woman married to a son of a bitch like him, you'd have to find somethin' to keep your mind occupied too. Those lads we caught last night didn't care for old Rigdon at all, an' I've found out that when you know folks real well and don't have much of an opinion of them, other folks can't go too far wrong makin' the same judgment."

"I wonder if Cap caught up with the wagons?" Hoskins asked. "Them prisoners said his sons wasn't with him up there."

Knight was reaching for the jug again when he offered his opinion about that. "If they got a lick of sense, them an' anyone else includin' Missus Rigdon, they're on fast horses out of the country an' won't even look back for a week."

Colby and Amilie came through the front door. Both the men in the kitchen turned, stood in silent appraisal for a moment, then exchanged a furtive look. Amilie in poor light didn't look much like a grown woman. Not until she pre-ceded Colby into the kitchen where the light was marginally better was it obvious that she was indeed a woman. Not only a lithe, leggy, pretty woman, but someone who took imme-diate affront at what Ace Hoskins was doing at the stove.

She barely got through the introductions before shoulder-ing him away from the cooking. He did not offer very much resistance, but he rolled his eyes in an inquiring look at Ashe Colby. Like many men of his time and environment, his knowledge of females was limited to an occasional hooraw in some town. When it came right down to carrying on a conversation with them, or understanding them, or even knowing exactly how to react to them, Hoskins typified his kind of frontiersman. He was unalterably settled in a convic-tion founded upon ignorance and masculine superiority. He had lived that way and he would die that way.

CHAPTER 14

A Time for Rest

AMILIE was an excellent cook. Even Ace Hoskins admitted that, but not within her hearing. He waited until they had finished gorging and she had gone out back to the well for a bucket of water before he said it.

Colby's reaction was to gravely nod as though part of the credit was his. Anything having to do with Amilie had by now become a personal matter with him.

Henry Knight yawned, then said, "Well, how long you been up here?"

Colby replied in a general way. "About a week." He told them how he'd been captured and asked if they'd had anyone up north watching for his heliograph signal.

Hoskins repled. "Yep. Cap figured the four Rangers he sent up the road pretendin' to be rangemen lookin' for work would be spotted for Rangers right away. They was to make a camp below St. George until they saw your signal, then head south an' bring along with 'em anyone who was followin' them." Hoskins smiled slyly. "It worked like clockwork. With renegades shaggin' behind 'em they was able to mirror-signal southward where we was comin' in from the west."

Colby nodded. "An' what about those four men?"

Hoskins and Knight broadly smiled as Hoskins answered. "The rest of us was north of the Rigdon place. We read their signal as they moped along, and Cap took most of the company an' rode up there. He'll have to tell you the rest. Me'n Henry was left down here to wait."

"Wait for what?"

Hoskins and Knight exchanged an ironic look. Knight got up, left the kitchen, was gone about ten minutes, and returned with one of those brass-bound, heavy oaken bullion boxes stage companies hauled gold and cash in. The hasp was broken, so he had no trouble raising the lid.

Colby arose to stare at the bundles of greenbacks tied with green yarn. At this moment Amilie trudged in with the bucket of water. She saw the box, put the bucket down, and walked over. Without seeming either awed at the amount of money, or surprised to see the box, she said, "You gents must have been here since yesterday to have finally found it."

Knight fixed her with a chilly gaze. "You knew about it?"

"Yes. One time about three years ago when Mister Rigdon developed a phobia about the house catchin' afire his wife told me he got crazy notions every now an' then an' not to pay any attention, he'd be off on something different next month.

"I was scrubbin' the floor in the hall an' saw the box on his bed. He wasn't around. When I went back that evenin' the box was gone." Amilie turned back for the bucket as she finished her recitation. "I knew it had to be in his room because he didn't take it outside with him when he left the house." She hoisted the bucket to a stove burner. "Where did you find it?"

Knight answered. "Under the grate in that iron stove in his bedroom, covered with kindling."

"I thought that had to be about where he'd hid it, because he wouldn't light a fire in there, even when it was downright cold in the house."

Colby selected several greenbacks and felt them. He could no more identify counterfeit money from sound money than most other people could, if the counterfeits were good ones.

But Henry Knight could. He too selected a note, stretched it between both hands, and held it to the lamp. "See them little colored threads in the paper, Ashe? Well now, wait a minute."

Knight fished in a pocket for a crumpled greenback and held it to the light in the same way. "See any little threads?"

Colby shook his head and Knight smiled broadly as he tossed the second greenback in front of Colby. "That one's counterfeit. Pretty good though, by golly. I got it off one of the men we captured yesterday evening."

Colby eased gently back down on his chair seat, staring at the bullion box. "That is sound money?" he asked, and when Hoskins and Knight inclined their heads, Colby said, "How much is there?"

They hadn't counted it. "A lot. When Cap gets back he can count it an' be responsible for it." Knight asked Amilie if there was any coffee left. When she brought the pot over and filled his cup, he studied her until she was moving to fill the other cups, then he said, "They'll be along, won't they?"

Her head came up. "Who?"

"You know who; Rigdon's boys. They'll be back for this box, won't they?"

Amilie put the pot down, straightened back, and speared Henry Knight with a defiant glare. "How would I know? Elizabeth told me about it, but I don't know whether the boys knew about it or not."

Knight's gaze drifted around to Colby, then back to the girl. He smiled at her when he said, "Couple of them prisoners told us you'n the youngest Rigdon was sweet on each other."

Colby started to arise but Amilie's laughter stopped him. She told Hoskins and Knight the story she'd told him about Samuel Rigdon trying to kiss her in the barn and his mother whaling the daylights out of him with her basket full of eggs. When she'd finished, she looked Henry Knight straight in the eye and said, "Did Ashe tell you about my little nickel-plated gun?"

Henry nodded.

"I didn't tell Ashe why I kept it loaded and oiled. If Sam'l ever tried that again I was goin' to kill him. Mister, does that sound like I was sweet on him?"

Knight raised a finger to scratch the tip of his nose as he replied. "No, ma'am, it sure don't. I mentioned what them captives said to see your reaction. I been at this business a long time. I can read faces pretty well."

"Can you," Amilie fired back. "And what did you read in my face just now?"

Knight grinned. "That them captives was liars."

She went back to her work at the stove. Colby asked where the captives were and how many they had. Knight's reply surprised him.

"Under guard an' in irons out at their money-makin' soddy. We caught eight, two got away, and while Cap's up yonder after them wagons to fetch the evidence back down here before they can get it over the line into Utah, me'n Ace was supposed to wait for someone to come back for Rigdon's strongbox. But it's daylight now." Knight sipped coffee before also saying, "Maybe they'll try it in broad daylight if they don't figure anyone's here, but I wouldn't. Not for twice this much money. Not when a company of Arizona Rangers is runnin' loose, armed for bear an' lookin' for trouble." Knight pushed the empty cup aside. "But then I'm not one of the Rigdons."

He arose, reset his hat, jerked his head at Hoskins, and started toward the front of the house. The sun was not very high but it was climbing. The heat which would arrive later was still in abeyance. There were animals in the barn requiring care.

As Colby was arising to follow the older men, Amilie turned from the dishpan, sleeves above her elbows, and looked at him. "I keep thinkin' of Elizabeth. She never approved. She never came right out and told me that, but over the years I got to know, to understand her." Amilie reached for a gray towel to dry her hands. "I could have cried for Elizabeth a hundred times. Right now too. Where is she? What will happen to her? Ashe, the only one she tried to care for an' protect was Sam'l. She was still tryin' to shield him from what was goin' on even after he was as much a part of it as her oldest son an' her man.

"I know she cried. Sometimes when we were alone here, I'd hear her in the kitchen or in her bedroom. Ashe, you don't owe me anything, but all the same, if they find Elizabeth, please help her."

He smiled. "I will. Do you have any idea where she went?"

"No. I'd guess she'd try to get up to St. George where Arizona law couldn't touch her. I expect most of them will. That's about all that's left unless they want to go to prison, isn't it?"

He thought it was. "I expect so. I'll be back directly."

She stood in the kitchen doorway watching him leave the house in the direction of the barn, then turned slowly back to her work. The only thing that reminded her of old Sid was that open box full of sound money on the kitchen table. Everything else reminded her of the woman who, in her own bitter and disillusioned way, had been good to Amilie.

The morning was progressing, heat was beginning to build up, and the land as far as Colby could see in any direction was empty.

While he and the older men were doing chores at the barn and keeping a casual watch over the countryside, Colby told them of the attack on the wagons, of the man with the ivory-handled gun named McKenna, and of Porter Hanson, Jethro, and the others who had been on hand when Colby and Amilie had been caught the last time.

There were many things to be discussed among the three of them. As time passed and the morning wore along, it was possible for Colby to fit all the pieces into a mosaic that made sense.

For one thing, he knew Captain Frank Hauser very well. If Hauser had triumphed at that wagon-fight, he would probably return southward to either the soddy or the Rigdon place, but if he was bringing the wagons back with him, it might be hours before he arrived. Possibly not until evening, if then. But whatever he did about the wagons and their incriminating freight, the prisoners he had taken during that angry encounter up yonder, he would not stop his manhunt until he was satisfied everything had been done that could be done.

Henry Knight and Ace Hoskins solemnly agreed with Colby about this. They knew the hardheaded, unrelenting chief Ranger.

What interested Hoskins was how and when they would leave this country. He did not even mention crossing back through the reservation the way Colby had got up here, and if they used the stage road it would not only take days to reach Rosalia and their barracks, it would also require constant vigilance because, as Hoskins pointed out, regardless of how hard they rode or how diligent they were in manhunting, this counterfeiting organization was too large and was spread over too much territory for one raid to catch everyone who was involved in it.

It was Hoskins's opinion that if they returned by the stage road the angry and vengeful people they had not caught—who were notoriously successful ambushers—would make trouble somewhere down the line.

They were sitting in the cool barn having a rambling discussion when one of the stalled horses pushed his head out as far as he could above the lower door, looked out back, and whinnied.

All three men came up to their feet in an instant. The horse was straining to see something out of his line of vision to the west.

Henry Knight made a drawling comment. "Well, well, well. I was beginnin' to think we was bein' left out of everything." He waited until Hoskins had gone to the rear opening to look past shadows into sunsmash, then said, "See anything?"

Hoskins turned, shaking his head, then turned back and

moved into shadows at the north side of the opening, where very little of his body was visible. "It's a band of horses," he called, "back up the runway."

"Who's drivin' them?"

"No one as far as I can see. Hey, Ashe, they got wild horses around here?"

Colby hadn't heard of any. "I don't know."

Hoskins called again. "Hell of a lot of dust an' they're quite a ways off. Come have a look."

The horses were coming up from the southwest and were running on a northeasterly course. They would pass the yard about a mile out. Dust rose above them, making a count impossible, but as Hoskins had said, it was a whole band.

Knight watched in silence for a long time, eyes narrowed. "That's not wild horses," he said matter-of-factly. "That's someone's remuda. Watch in back. That damned dust is thick enough to plow, but there's got to be someone behind them."

He was right, but not until the herd had come abreast of the barn and was streaking past was it possible to make out a mounted man in the drag, bandana covering most of his face to protect him from the dust.

He did not look to his right, the direction of the Rigdon yard. He was concentrating on keeping the horses moving. Knight and Hoskins raised questioning expressions, but Colby shook his head. The rider was too distant for identification, but it was beginning to cross Colby's mind that this might be one of the local stockmen bringing in his remuda. There was no reason to feel uneasy, particularly since the drive did not slacken pace nor did its drover show interest in the Rigdon place.

The noise was distantly audible. If the drive had been closer, its passing would have made more than enough noise to prevent the men inside the barn from hearing anything else, but it was not that close, so when the abrupt shattering of glass over at the house overrode the more distant, muffled sound of running horses, Colby spun toward the front door-way with Hoskins and Knight coming around at the same time.

By the time they got up there, the suspicion that those running horses had been a deliberate ruse to hold their attention away from the house was in each man's mind.

CHAPTER 15

Mano y Mano

IT was a good guess, but they did not realize it because there was no sign of men or horses over there, and people occasionally and accidentally broke windows.

Knight exchanged a look with Ace Hoskins; they were like a pair of hunting dogs, they transmitted thoughts by eye. Knight said, "You go out the back way and try'n keep sheds between you'n the house. I'll try goin' around the north end an' over to the opposite sheds."

Hoskins was turning away when Colby stopped him. "The money box was on the kitchen table."

Hoskins nodded and walked away. Henry Knight leaned in barn gloom watching the front of the house until his companion was away from the barn, then he straightened up and wagged his head. "If Cap finds out we was careless with that cache he'll peg our hides to the side of the barn. Ashe, who d'you expect they might be?"

It was not an answerable question but Colby tried anyway. "Maybe the men you'n Ace were supposed to watch for."

Knight nodded, still watching the front of the house. "Sam'l an' Joseph. They had a friend, though, didn't they? The feller who drove that remuda past."

Colby nodded. "And maybe more. If you try to cross the yard up north they'll catch you sure as hell."

Knight had no chance to reply. A flurry of gunshots erupted from the west side of the house, back where old Sidney's bedroom was. Colby and Knight ran to the rear of the barn in time to see Ace Hoskins flattened against a thick-

119

walled smokehouse unable to go back or forward. Colby swore. "They got eyes like eagles."

Knight, satisfied his friend would not be wounded, remarked about something else. "I guess that let the cat out of the bag, an' from the racket, sure as hell, it's more'n just one man."

When the firing ended and the echoes had chased each other into oblivion, the silence returned, deeper this time and more ominous.

Knight's jaw muscles rippled as they returned to the front of the barn. He was angry with himself for abandoning the bullion box. When Colby thought aloud that the men in the house would be able to escape through the rear of the house, which would put the house between them and the men down by the barn, Knight swore fiercely before saying, "Over my carcass." He marched to the rear of the barn to see if Hoskins was still behind the smokehouse. He was, and he grimaced at Knight.

Up front Colby was worrying about Amilie. As surely as the Good Lord made little green apples, the men in the house would use her as a shield when they fled, and that would prevent Colby from doing anything even if he could get ahorseback and go after them.

When Knight returned, Colby said, "Mexican standoff," but the older man would not accept that either.

"They left their horses out back. No other way they could have got in there. Ashe, those are pretty damned coyote fellers. How'd they know to sneak around in back?"

Colby's answer was matter-of-fact. "Smoke from the kitchen stove. I wondered about that when Ace fired it up. Smoke stands straight up in the still early morning. They'd see it from a couple of miles out."

Knight said nothing as he stood in barn gloom, invisible from the house, watching the front of the building. Only when there was a sound of muted commotion over there did he rouse himself. "We got to get around back and chouse their horses off."

Colby was willing. "How?"

"Come along. I'll show you. Bring that big bay horse on a shank. I'll take the one nearest the back doorway."

The ruse was not original. A man could cross open country with a horse between himself and other men. It was frequently fatal to horses but not always.

As Colby and Knight were leaving the barn, they looked southward. Hoskins was no longer behind the smokehouse and that worried his friends, who grumbled about a damned fool taking chances. But as far as Colby could see, there was no other way for Hoskins to get away from the smokehouse, or even return to the barn, without taking chances.

North of the barn was an equipment shed which had three sides and an open front. Inside was a dray wagon, a battered topbuggy, and a ranch runabout that had springs under the seat and nowhere else. Each vehicle had its shafts or tongue propped atop small wooden barrels.

Beyond the equipment shed there was just one additional structure, a rough-made log bunkhouse with a dilapidated old privy behind it. After that there was open country to the north for miles, while eastward across the upper end of the yard were several more outbuildings including another three-sided structure with soot inside it on walls, ceiling, and even the earthen floor. It was a blacksmithing shed.

The horses fidgeted. Knight growled at them as he studied the distance to be crossed. Behind him Colby said, "Hundred an' fifty feet. Maybe two hundred."

Knight nodded without being diverted from his study. "What's that shack directly across from us?"

Colby had no idea, but it looked to be a granary, at least someone had clearly taken great pains to caulk the places where mice could get inside. "It don't matter what it is," he told Knight. "It's the nearest one." Colby listened, then blew out a big breath. It would help like hell if Hoskins, wherever he was, would start a ruckus near the house. But that did not appear likely.

Knight said, "You ready?"

Colby responded drily. "No, but standin' here don't do any good either."

Knight drew his six-gun, let it hang at his side, made a final appraisal of the ground to be covered without protection, and said, "Let's go!"

Both horses had languished in stalls too long. They were almost too eager, and as though sensing the urgency of the men, they lunged ahead. Knight swore at his horse; it tried to break away, and in yanking its head around the horse's body interfered with his forward movement. He yanked on the shank and turned the air blue.

Behind him Colby's animal was only slightly less fractious. Neither man looked southward in the direction of the house.

They were halfway across toward the granary when a man's excited yell rang into the stillness. Colby slapped his animal. Ahead of him, Knight had stopped swearing and was trotting as his animal pulled him along.

They were two-thirds of the way when a shot sounded. Neither man knew where the slug struck. They were hastening toward salvation, mouths open as they sucked air, eyes fixed on the granary.

They made it. There was no gunfire after that solitary shot. Colby pulled his excited beast toward a protruding low eave and tied it there. The horse pulled back, but the rope held and the eave was solidly unmovable.

Knight was looking for something to tie his animal to when there was a ragged burst of gunfire from the house. He scowled and looked inquiringly at his companion, but Colby had no idea what that fusillade had been about either. It was certainly not aimed in their direction, because they hadn't been in sight for a couple of minutes.

Knight said, "Ace!" He was probably right but there was no way to be sure. The firing stopped; blending with the echoes was the unmistakable sound of running horses. Knight blurted words out. "They're escaping. The god-damned money's gone." He began fashioning a squaw bridle of the lead rope to the horse he'd used as a shield. His clear intention was to spring aboard and ride in pursuit with no bridle, saddle, and with only a handgun.

Colby yelled at him. "Wait!"

He might just as well have tried to stop a whirlwind. Knight was turning the horse to him so he could swing up when someone down at the house bellowed like a bay steer and fired wildly with a six-gun.

Knight stopped, looked southward, then looked at his companion. Colby was moving along the north wall of the granary. When he reached the corner he removed his hat, knelt, and eased his face around. Whoever had made that enraged bawl of sound and had fired his weapon empty was not only silent now but there was no sighting of him.

There was something else, though: vague signs of move-ment beyond a broken window. Colby remained kneeling for a long time before returning to the rear of the building where Knight was waiting. "Well," the older man snapped.

Colby had been considering an idea as he walked back. "They're still in the house. At least some of them are. There was movement."

Knight looked blank.

"I think Ace got around yonder and turned their horses loose."

Knight blinked, turned slowly to begin a stalk behind the east-side outbuildings, and did not say a word until he was forced to halt because of open country between the last outbuilding and the main house. Then he turned and said, "Let that be a lesson to you younger fellers. Us old dogs know more ways to skin a cat than you can shake a stick at."

Colby nodded in solemn agreement without believing one word Knight had said. Hoskins couldn't have used any tricks to get around the house without using normal precaution and mastering a gutful of courage.

Maybe it amounted to the same thing. Colby eased up past the older man, got flat down, and poked his head around the last outbuilding at ground level. He had an excellent view of the house. There was heat on his back, which he was unaware of, and there was a bluish, dancing haze far out, which he was also unaware of.

Knight said, "What's behind the house? Is there a place for Ace to hide?"

There were several places back there a man could hide; the most obvious one was the outhouse, but anyone coyote enough to sneak around in back and put the men inside the house on foot would not use such an obvious hideout.

Colby did not reply. He was trying to catch sight of someone, anyone, inside the house, but the longer he watched without seeing anyone, the more uneasy he became. He was about half ready to believe there was no one in there when Knight swore. "Goddammit, we left the barn unguarded."

Colby rolled back and came up to his feet. There were still two horses in the stalls. He was sure there were more than two men opposing them. Knight was turning back when he said, "I'll get up where I can see down the runway. You stay here."

Colby shrugged as he watched the older man retrace his steps. Without warning a man bellowed from the house. In the still air his words carried far beyond the yard, but what impressed Colby was the notion that he recognized that voice and knew its owner. He would have bet his life on it. There was a very good chance that he damned well might do exactly that!

"Hey! You fellers in the yard! We got a trade for you!" The caller paused before continuing. "Saddled horses for the girl! No horses, we shoot the girl!"

Colby leaned against the building. If he'd had time to

reflect, he would have come to the conclusion that this situation was bound to arrive—after Hoskins had choused off the animals tethered behind the house.

Like the older men, he had been through hostage situations before, but dispassionately, never with personal involvement.

Henry Knight's recognizable voice called back with a solid ring of gloating. "You harm the girl an' you not only won't get no horses, we'll hang you from the barn rafters!"

Colby continued to lean in shade, watching the house. For a long while there was no sound from the house. The next shout was from Knight, not the man with the bull-bass voice at the house.

"You can come out unarmed or you can set in there an' stew until the rest of the company gets down here, but mister, you don't get away from here with that money. Not if we got to keep you in there for a damned year."

The silence ran on. It appeared to Colby that the men in the house hadn't expected such defiance, but then they did not know the position they had put Knight in when they'd found that bullion box on the kitchen table. Nor did they know Henry Knight, whose temperament was as unyielding as stone in this kind of situation.

But they did have an ace: Amilie.

Unexpectedly, someone fired a carbine from inside the front of the barn. The report was higher, more waspish than the report of a handgun. To Colby's knowledge, neither of the older men had a carbine—and he certainly didn't.

Three ragged return-shots peeled slivers of wood and dust from the front of the barn near the doorway. The carbine-man over there evidently did not go farther back, because he levered up and fired three times as fast as he could, and this time Colby heard howls inside the house.

Knight yelled again, his voice as defiant and threatening as before. To Colby, he sounded like someone who had the advantage.

"You're goin' to get yourselves killed. Take my word for it, you sons of bitches! You come out standin' up or we'll drag you out by the ankles!"

Colby thought that was unnecessarily harsh talk for someone who not only lacked the protection their enemies had, but who didn't even know how badly he, Colby, and Hoskins were outnumbered.

Again, there was no immediate response, but it eventually came. It was the same voice, this time with a bullying edge to it which convinced Colby again that he knew the man.

"How many of you fellers is out there?"

Knight's fierce belligerence had convinced the men in the house they had to bargain. When Knight replied, Colby shook his head. Knight should have lied, but he didn't.

"Three right now and ten or twelve on the way."

This time Colby would have bet his mule-nosed horse he knew the owner of the responding voice. Not just from its sound but from the man's response to Knight.

The voice was harsh, bitter and curt. Colby could visualize its owner standing wide-legged, utterly without fear, his right hand lying lightly atop a holstered Colt with ivory grips.

McKenna!

"Man to man! You step out into the yard an' I'll come out onto the porch. Man to man, you hollerin' bastard! Whichever one's still standin' gets the money, the girl, and gets the horses to ride away. Hey; you hear me?"

Colby reacted before Knight had a chance to. "If you go down, how about your friends in there?"

"They won't do anything. We already talked it over. You scairt?"

Colby raised and lowered Hanson's gun in its old holster. He called to the older men. "Henry! Ace! Man to man. Keep out of it."

Knight protested. "You're crazy. We don't have to do this. They're not goin' nowhere and Cap'll be along directly."

Colby's reply was as hard as stone. "Yeah, I got to do it. I know him. I owe it to him. Just keep out of it!"

CHAPTER 16

Gunsmoke

McKENNA had asked scornfully whether Colby was afraid. Yes, indeed, he was afraid. Only a madman, an absolute fool, or a seasoned and supremely confident killer would not have been.

Colby tested Hanson's weapon and holster several more times without replying to the gunman.

Knight yelled toward the house. "What's this goin' to settle? We don't have to face you down. You can't get five miles on foot an' by sundown there'll be a swarm of us after you."

McKenna, made more confident than ever by Knight's protest, taunted the men he could not see. "Yaller? Got a foot-wide yaller strip down your back, have you? Even yaller-bellies can act brave from hiding. I give you the challenge an' you took it. Now keep your word."

Colby reset his hat, wiped sweat from the palms of his hands, and faced the house. "Come ahead. When you walk out I'll be there."

This time the gunman said, "All right. An' let me tell you somethin', mister. If them friends of yours even look like they're going to shoot, my friends in here'll blow them to kingdom come—and the girl!"

Knight started to make a derisive comment about that, but Colby cut in, saying, "Keep out of it, Henry! An' keep your word. If he wins, they ride out. Remember that!"

From inside the barn a man called loudly, his voice sounding as though it came from a cave. "Ashe! Henry's right.

You're crazy. We don't have to make no trades with 'em. Ashe? You hear me? It's Hoskins. Wait 'em out. I ran off their horses. They're afoot an' Cap'll be along directly."

The advice was sound, but what neither Knight nor Hoskins knew was that Colby had developed a fierce hatred for the arrogant man with the ivory-stocked gun. When he called to Knight and Hoskins for the last time, he said, "Just keep out of it! It's somethin' personal."

That silenced the older men. It required no great amount of prescience to realize there was already bad blood between the challenger and the man who had accepted the challenge.

The taunting voice called once more from the house before the door opened. "Your momma's goin' to be cryin' tonight."

When McKenna stepped out to the porch, right hand inches from the gun he wore, it was quiet enough to hear a bird call from far out somewhere. He looked taller and thicker up there than he'd looked before. And he was smiling up around narrowed, probing eyes.

Colby moved around into sight. McKenna watched him walk toward the middle of the yard, and as he started down off the porch he said, "How'd you get free?"

Colby did not reply. He halted near the center of the yard, watching McKenna stroll toward him from the house. When the gunfighter halted, took his stance, and continued to smile, Colby said, "You've already lost. The Rangers got the wagons. They got prisoners too."

McKenna continued to grin. "That's all right, cowboy. After we heard the fight up yonder I figured it was all over."

"You should have gone up to St. George instead of coming down here. What took you so long to get here anyway?"

McKenna almost imperceptibly moved his fingers until they brushed the graceful sweep of his weapon as he said, "I got enemies up in St. George. When I get across the reservation southward, I'll be free as a bird. Besides, after I left the pueblo last night I come onto Sam'l and Joseph. We went to pick up some others before comin' here to find the old man's strongbox. . . . Cowboy, you want to talk? We can get a couple of chairs if you do."

Colby breathed deeply, watching for the slightest flicker of movement in the man who was about a hundred feet from him. A slight sound from the house almost distracted Colby, but not quite; instinct told him this had been planned. He had a fraction of a second to react to what he instinctively knew was supposed to follow that disconcerting sound, and went for his holster.

The gunshots were no more than a couple of seconds apart. Too short a length of time to influence either shooter.

Colby felt nothing. He wouldn't have anyway, even if one of his legs had been cut off. Every nerve, muscle, and thought was heightened into total concentration on what he was doing. He hauled the hammer back for the second shot and saw his adversary doing the same, but with a hair's-breadth moment of fatal delay. He also saw McKenna's shirt blossom scarlet when the gunfighter moved very slightly as Colby tugged off his second shot, which was followed by McKenna's second shot, and that time Colby did not feel pain but he felt the air leaving his body. He opened his mouth but no air returned.

McKenna's gun hand wilted. The gunfighter made a fierce attempt to steady it on the rise, but the damage was too great. His muscles would have responded but not his nerves; shock had paralyzed them.

Knight was yelling. "Again, boy, again!"

Colby was tightening his bent finger inside the trigger guard with the hammer pulled back when McKenna's gun fell to the ground. He stood like a lightning-struck tree looking steadily at the man who had shot him.

Knight was quiet. So was everyone else. So was that distant bird who'd been calling a few minutes earlier. Only the sun moved, so slowly it seemed not to be moving at all.

They fell, but exactly as they had fired, one falling a second or two before the other one fell.

From the house, a shocked man called into the silence. "That was his idea, you sons of bitches. We told him it was crazy, but no one ever told McKenna anything. Now he's out of it an' we still got the girl an' the money."

For the first time Knight was unable to yell his defiance. Hoskins called from the barn. "Truce until we get Ashe out of the sun?"

That same slightly nasal, shocked voice answered. "Like hell. You saddle them horses an' tie 'em out front, then you'n your friend start walkin' north where we can keep watch and leave your weapons behind. You hear me?"

Hoskins said a startling word of monumental disgust before bitterly reminding the forted-up men of the agreement before the gunfight. His only answer was a sound of disdainful laughter.

The silence returned, the sun burned down, a thirsty horse behind Hoskins in the barn began to fretfully strike his stall door with a hoof, and out where the two men were lying, the silence was shattered by a woman's keening high wail.

Henry Knight had been moving stealthily during Hoskins's exchange with the men inside the house. When he got back down where Colby had been standing, with no protection between this site and the house, he paused to push sweat off with a soiled cuff and squint fiercely toward the building.

He'd been lucky once when he'd crossed the yard. Instinct told him he would not be lucky again, but he balanced there unreasonably furious and therefore incapable of rational thought.

A wisp of a shadow passed behind the shattered window, moving with almost fluid grace. Knight fired without more than tipping his gun barrel. The wispy form went wildly sideways and someone screamed inside the house.

The gunfire erupted again, searching this time and furious. Knight flattened around behind his building, shucked out the spent casing, plugged in a fresh load, and pushed off more sweat. He felt better. It had been too fast a shot to be accurate without luck, but evidently the luck had been there.

When the firing dwindled, both Knight and Hoskins had made a tally. Hoskins thought there had been five men firing and Knight thought there were four, but both were satisfied that there were now two less, one of them visibly dead and the other one either in the same state or, they hoped, hit hard enough to be out of the fight.

Hoskins yelled again. "All right; you want to go—walk out back an' go. Leave the money an' go!"

This time when the voice replied it was different. It was brusque and practical. "One of you lead them horses over here an' we'll leave."

If either of the older men derived any satisfaction from this clear evidence that the men at the house'd had enough, they gave no indication of it, especially Henry Knight, who now became even more demanding. "Send the girl out with the strongbox an' we'll talk about givin' you the horses."

Again there was a long lull. Knight was spitting cotton, less from the heat than from thirst caused by too much agitation, too much agitated sweating.

The brusque voice called back, making the first real concession. "All right. She's comin' out, but she can't carry the box."

Knight sounded derisive when he yelled back. "Why not, it's not heavy. That's paper money, not silver or gold."

"Because," the other man replied, "she's got a busted arm."

Knight was silent so long Hoskins over in the barn did not think he'd reply. But he finally did. "What happened to her arm?"

The brusque voice replied shortly. "You want her or don't you?"

"Send her out."

"Your word about the horses."

Knight spat, glared, and almost choked over his reply. "Yeah, my word. An' it's better than yours. Send her out."

Someone opened the door from behind it. Amilie came out a little unsteadily and blinked in the sunlight. One arm was shoved in the front of her shirt, with the other arm supporting it at the elbow.

Knight was about to call to her to head for the barn when she went down the stairs and, without looking left or right, went directly past McKenna and dropped to her knees beside Ashe Colby, her sobs audible to everyone who was watching.

Amilie raised Colby's head to her lap and one-handedly wiped dust from his face, bent over to shield him from direct sunlight, and gently rocked as she cried, reminding Hoskins and Knight of the way Indian squaws acted in similar situations.

She stopped rocking, bent lower, then straightened back and looked around as she said, "Water! Please, someone, water. He's alive!"

Hoskins replied to her. "I dassn't bring it to you, but there's a canteen in the barn. Can you make it?"

She eased Colby's head to the ground, turned his face away from direct sunlight, got unsteadily to her feet, and started walking.

Hoskins went after a canteen and was waiting when she walked into the gloom. He was shocked at her appearance. Someone with fists like granite had worked her over. One eye was almost closed, there was a stain of blood at the corner of a swollen underlip, her eyes were much darker than usual, their expression full of pain. He handed her the canteen, watched her turn back toward the center of the yard, and picked up the carbine he'd taken from the rig on one of the horses he'd turned loose. His expression was murderous.

The stillness continued as Amilie knelt beside Colby and trickled water into his mouth. When he swallowed, she made a lopsided smile, then dampened a bandana and wiped his face. When he looked up at her, tears spilled on his cheeks.

She said, "Lie still."

"Where is it, Amilie? Where am I hit?"

All she knew was that his lower body was covered with sticky blood. "Lie still. As soon as I can, I'll take care of you."

"Amilie? What happened to you? Did McKenna do that?"

"No, Joseph."

"He's in the house?"

She nodded. "They both are. Joseph and Sam'l."

"Who else?"

"Two other men. I've seen them before but I don't know their names. Ashe, don't move. Drink more water. I'll see if they'll let me get you out of the sun."

They wouldn't. When she appealed to the men in the house, the man with the brusque voice snarled his answer. "The horses. You fellers out there keep your word. Saddle them horses an' fetch them over to the front of the house. Amilie . . . get out of the yard. You're in the way. You hear me, girl?"

Knight snarled loudly. "Leave her be. You'll get your horses. Ace?"

"All right. I'll saddle 'em."

Knight put up his weapon, spat more cotton, and went trudging northward up where he and Colby had left the animals they'd used as shields earlier. Without those two, there would not be enough horses for the men in the house.

CHAPTER 17

Dead Men

UNHEEDED by the participants of the fight in the Rigdon ranch yard, the sun had reached its meridian and was now on the down side. The heat remained, and for the men in the house at least, there was drinking water. For Henry Knight the need ended as he was trudging up where the horses were tied. He kicked open the rear door of a building which had evidently served as a cookshack when the Rigdons had been in the cattle business, found water in there, drank his fill, splashed water over his head and shirt, and returned to the yard where sunlight hit him in the face as he looked northward.

He squinted, surprised that it was much later in the day than he would have assumed, spat, and continued up where the horses were standing in the building shade.

Across the yard Ace Hoskins had two horses saddled and was standing back in semigloom watching Amilie as she crooned while using a damp bandana to do what she could for Ashe Colby. Hoskins's leashed fury was visible in the expression on his face when he heard Knight call from across the yard northward, and turned in that direction.

"Watch the house," Knight called, reasonably sure the forted-up men would not shoot but unwilling to lead the horses into plain sight without making certain that if they did start firing, someone wouldn't be in position to provide a diversion. Hoskins had that rapid-firing carbine, and he was a good shot.

Knight was right, there were no gunshots as he crossed

open ground, walking between the horses, expecting them to be as fractious as they had been earlier. But they were perfectly content to be led along, probably because of thirst.

He went down the back of the barn, invisible to the men who were watching from the south end of the yard, whistled to warn Hoskins he was coming, and entered the barn with the horses.

Hoskins arose from one knee with the carbine in his hands. He leaned the weapon aside to help with the horses. As they were working to rig them out, Hoskins said, "I'm goin' to kill that son of a bitch who beat the girl if I got to take a leave an' track him for a year."

Knight's mood was no different. "You won't have to track him. We'll hang him from the rafters, up where them owl droppings are."

As they were finishing with the horses, Hoskins said, "They're not goin' to give us a chance, Henry. You heard 'em; we're to walk northward unarmed. Except for the girl I wouldn't do this. I don't care who gave their word. The situation'll be reversed, we'll be afoot and they'll be mounted. With that damned money."

Knight was bitter and cranky. "They'll leave the girl. The condition she's in, she'd slow 'em down. As for the money— I was lookin' for work when Cap hired me an' I can look for it again."

Hoskins cocked his head. Knight had sounded defeated. But he said nothing because someone yelled from the house, "What the hell's takin' so long? Get them horses up here!"

Hoskins leaned across a saddle seat looking at his companion. Knight was drenched with sweat. "I don't care if they got a Gatling gun in there, they've gone as far as they're goin' to go, but we got to take care of Ashe, he needs us more'n Cap needs them renegades or that money."

Knight raised his hat, pushed sweat off with a grimy sleeve, dropped the hat back down, and eyed his friend from a distance of about fifteen feet. "Yeah. But right now we're losin', not winning."

Hoskins nodded and stepped back to pick up some reins and start walking. He was almost to the front opening when Knight said, "You got any empties in your six-gun, because I'll bet you a new horse when they tell us to start walkin' northward after they make us shuck our guns, we're goin' to get shot in the back."

Hoskins halted and looked back. "Henry, Ashe Colby an' the girl are out there in the middle of the yard, they'll—"

"They'll kill them too."

"Damn it, let me finish. They're out in the yard an' I got no empties in my gun, an' I didn't come down in the last rain, I know what they'll do. An' I know somethin' else. When you follow me out of here, you stick your six-gun in the back of your britches so's they'll see empty holsters an' when they come out of the house you'n me'll start shooting across saddle seats, an' keep right on shootin' until we're shot out. You got a better notion?"

Knight was grinning as he lifted the gun from his holster, shoved it in back, and wagged his head at Ace Hoskins. As he led his horses along he said, "Ace, you ever know anybody who lived forever?"

Hoskins was in sunlight and neither answered nor took his eyes off the front of the house, except once, as he walked past Amilie and Colby; he smiled winterly at the girl and said, "Make him hang on."

Knight trudged by without even saying that much. Ahead of them where shadows were beginning to form along the front of the house, a man called exultantly. "They're comin', Joseph." If Colby had heard the voice, he would have known it belonged to Samuel Rigdon. Neither Hoskins nor Knight knew Samuel Rigdon; their only concern was that he had told his forted-up companions the horses were coming.

In the westerly distance a solitary rider appeared, riding at a dead walk. The men in the yard noticed this before

anyone from the house did, but neither of them said anything, did not in fact pay much attention to the distant rider
whose course was directly toward the yard.

Joseph Rigdon appeared in the broken window. He stood
impassively studying the men out front. He said, "Turn 'em
sideways; I want to see if you cut the cinchas."

Hoskins and Knight obeyed, being careful not to also turn
sideways as they pulled the animals around. Knight growled
at the man in the window. "We didn't cut 'em. Just get on the
horses an' let us get back yonder to look after our friend."

Joseph could have been deaf for all the indication he gave
that he'd heard Knight. From the corner of his mouth he
addressed someone behind him out of sight. "Go out there,
check the horses."

Knight was running sweat again. Hoskins was, too, but not
as profusely; a man neither of them recognized stepped out
of the house, Colt in hand, hovered briefly on the porch,
then started down toward the horses. Hoskins made a disgusted remark to the stranger. "You goin' to shoot a horse?
You don't need that gun. The horses are harmless an' so are
we."

The whisker-stubbled, tired-looking man from the house
approached each animal and not only pulled saddlehorns to
satisfy himself the saddles were snug, he also looked at the
reins. As he was turning to speak to the man in the window
he saw the approaching rider and pulled straight up for a
moment, then spoke to Joseph Rigdon.

"Rider comin' from the west."

Knight could have kissed the man. He'd been expecting
Joseph to order him and his partner to turn around. He'd
have seen those concealed guns if the oncoming horseman
hadn't captured his attention.

Joseph said, "Just one?"

His man nodded, still squinting. "Yeah. One's all I can see
anyway. Joseph, they been talkin' about more Rangers. We're
wastin' time."

Evidently Joseph agreed with this, because he left the window, growled an order in the house, and led the way out onto the porch. Hoskins and Knight had their first good look at the men they'd been trying to kill for half a day.

Neither of them knew Joseph, but each of them recognized the eldest of old Rigdon's sons to be the most dangerous of the men alternately looking at that distant figure with sunlight at his back—making both horse and rider look almost eerily smokelike—and the two filthy, haggard, stubbled, and bitter-eyed men down there with the horses.

Joseph shot one indifferent glance out where Amilie was sitting in the dust holding Colby's head in her lap, dropped his flinty gaze to Hoskins and Knight, and jerked his head to the man closest to him. "Sam'l, fetch the sack." They had stuffed the greenbacks from the bullion box into a croaker sack, which was lighter and easier to carry.

When Samuel returned to the house, Joseph hooked thumbs in his shell-belt and sneered. "You didn't have a chance right from the start," he told the men looking up at him from across saddle seats. Joseph spat into the dust before continuing to speak. "McKenna was a fool. I always figured he was. He knew it all. He killed seven men. No one could beat him. All you had to do to know that was ask him. An' there he lies."

A wiry man muttered from behind Joseph. "Gettin' closer, Joseph. He could be a scout for the rest of them Rangers."

Joseph turned to briefly watch the distant rider. When Samuel appeared, a flour sack slung over one shoulder, Joseph nodded, still with both thumbs hooked in his shell-belt, and that, as old hands such as Hoskins and Knight knew, was the time to start firing, when the men in front of them were anxious to get away, were thinking of nothing else, and their spokesman had both thumbs hooked in a belt.

They did as Colby had noticed before, they exchanged a brief glance, reached behind, and with two men on the steps, Joseph and his brother still on the porch, raised their weapons without haste, cocked them at the last minute, and when the Rigdon brothers reacted almost instantaneously to the sound of guns being cocked, both Knight and Hoskins squeezed off their first shots.

The horses jumped violently, broke away, and fled in different directions. Out in the middle of the yard Amilie also jumped. Colby struggled to get an elbow set to prop himself up with as one of the men on the steps went backward as though struck head-on by a giant fist. He hit his head on the riser behind and rolled sideways.

The second man on the steps was clawing at his weapon as he hurled himself forward and sideways.

Knight had ignored them all except Joseph. His bullet drove Joseph Rigdon back almost to the doorway and twisted him to the right. He was drawing his gun and stumbling when Knight's next slug tore a six-inch sliver of wood from the doorjamb.

Joseph had his gun rising when Knight ducked to one side as Hoskins fired at the man who had jumped clear of the steps. He too missed, but not by much. Dust spurted no more than six inches from his target, and the man squawked. He appeared to be completely terrified. He scrambled along the ground on his elbows, as though to crawl away. His eyes bulged and his mouth was open. The gun on his right side was still in its holster.

Samuel had dropped the flour sack and was reaching for his holster, eyes wide in delayed astonishment. This was one time when his brother's contempt seemed borne out; Samuel was slow-witted, not enough so to matter in most things, but in this situation, it was more than enough.

Hoskins shot him through the body.

Joseph was trying for another shot at Knight, who was continuing to crouch and move as he hauled back the hammer for his third shot. Their weapons exploded simultaneously. Knight went over backward, rolled twice, and failed in an effort to sit up. With iron-willed resolve he raised his right arm and fired one more time, and that shot hit Joseph two inches above the eyes and directly between them. He was dead before his gun went off with his body falling ahead, half on the porch, half off it. His bullet plowed a runnel of hardpan dirt that sent dust flying.

Samuel was sitting down, looking stupidly at blood on his left hand, unfired six-gun beside him on the floorboards.

The only surviving, uninjured man, who had been trying to crawl, was getting both legs positioned to spring up and run when Henry Knight's vision of him blurred, darkened, and Knight collapsed in the dust.

Ace Hoskins turned slowly, saw the survivor, saw his partner sprawled between them, then moved away to step over Knight, and as the terrified man saw him coming, he began to scream for mercy.

Hoskins stopped above the wild-eyed man, took deliberate aim with his cocked six-gun, and the screaming man's eyes rolled up, his noise stopped, he loosened all over and crumpled.

Hoskins continued to stand a moment longer before easing down the hammer as he turned looking for any threat, found only one man still alive in front of him—Samuel sitting up there too dumbfounded to be dangerous—and knelt beside Knight to ease him over onto his back.

Knight said, "Watch 'em, dammit."

Hoskins smiled through sweat and dust. "Where'd he hit you?"

"How'n hell would I know, except that I can't set up. Never mind that. Watch 'em."

"No one left to watch, Henry, but a big, simple-minded son of a bitch up there on the porch starin' at the blood comin' out of his belly."

"Rigdon?"

"Dead. You ought to know, you nailed him right between the horns."

"Where am I hit, Ace?"

Hoskins leaned back, ran a slow look down his friend's body, and said, "In the hip. Hold still. I'll try'n stop the bleeding."

Hoskins ignored everything but his friend. Knight's wound was gushing blood. The bullet seemed to have been deflected by bone and had turned outward, tearing a large hole in his left ham.

Hoskins worked grimly to plug the holes. He succeeded in staunching most of the bleeding but not all of it. A noise on the porch distracted him for a moment. Samuel was trying to get to his feet, using both hands, palms down, to push with. Hoskins snarled at him. "Stay down, you son of a bitch. An' kick that gun off the porch."

Samuel stopped struggling but made no move to kick the gun. He gazed at Hoskins from dull, bewildered eyes. He said, "You shot me."

Hoskins studied Samuel for a moment then went back to work on Knight, who spoke in a tired-sounding tone of voice. "Never mind. There's still one left."

But Hoskins continued to ignore Samuel, except to now and then shoot a look up where he had dragged himself to the front of the house and was sitting there, propped against the wall, eyes blank, mouth slack.

The flow of blood diminished gradually, which Hoskins attributed to his vigorous efforts to force it to stop, unaware that Knight's body had begun to create its own defense against the loss of blood by closing off as much of the source as it could.

Hoskins sat back on his heels looking at his old friend. He was unsure whether Knight could hear him or not, but he spoke anyway. "You'll be all right. An' you got that bastard. I'm proud of you."

He would have said more, but a gunshot sounded from out in the yard somewhere, making an unfamiliar noise. Behind Hoskins a man made a choking sound. Hoskins whipped around. That man he hadn't killed because the man had fainted was bending over very slowly, a six-gun dangling from one hand, his other hand pressing tightly to his upper body.

Hoskins watched the man fall flat down, then turned. Amilie was still on her knees out there beside Ashe Colby.

She was holding a little nickel-plated revolver in her right hand. She was supporting her gun-hand with the left hand for steady aim.

Colby spoke as loudly as he could. "He was goin' to blow your head off."

Hoskins nodded at the girl, then leaned over Knight again.

None of them had noticed the rider who had been approaching at a dead walk from the west with the descending sun to the rear until they heard the solid sound of a horse entering the yard where everything else was deathly silent. That rider hadn't moved out of a walk since they'd first seen him.

Hoskins eased up to his feet with Knight's blood on his trousers, his hands and arms, and ran one hand down a trouser leg as he began to reach for his hip-holster while turning.

The rider reined directly toward the porch and did not stop until Hoskins cocked and raised his weapon. The rider ignored everything, the menacing gun included, got stiffly down, and walked past Hoskins without even seeing him, mounted the steps, knelt beside Samuel, looked at him briefly, then bent forward sobbing.

It was Elizabeth Rigdon.

CHAPTER 18

With Darkness Coming

FOR dead-tired people in a degree of shock, it was difficult to carry Colby and Knight into the house and onto beds, particularly since one of them was already wobbly and could use only one arm, but they accomplished it while the sun continued its dispassionate descent. That thirsty horse in a stall was kicking his door more insistently than ever.

As Hoskins stood at the kitchen table with old Sidney's jug in his fist, Amilie washed blood off her hands and arms. He said, "Take a couple swallows of this."

She looked at him over her shoulder. "Do you know what's happening on the porch?"

He knew. He hoisted the jug, swallowed twice, and put the jug down hard enough to rattle the table. "There's nothing to be done," he told her, avoiding her stare. "That's Missus Rigdon?"

"Yes. And Sam'l was her baby."

"Well, there's nothing anyone can do for him, girl. He's gut-shot. Even the best doctor in the territory couldn't do anything."

The whiskey had an almost miraculous effect. Hoskins's color improved and his eyes brightened on Amilie. "I owe you."

Her reply was typical. "You wouldn't if you hadn't been so damned careless. Didn't you hear him movin' behind you?"

"No, ma'am. Excuse me, I'll go cut the clothes off Knight and Colby. You fetch some hot water an' clean rags when you're ready."

She stopped him in the doorway. He had old Sidney's jug hanging from his fingers. "Whiskey's not medicine," she told him, and he solemnly eyed her in silence for a moment before replying. "Back in Kentucky my grandma, who made mighty fine corn squeezings, told me the Good Lord made everythin' on this earth for a purpose, an' He knew, an' she knew, there wasn't nothin' better for someone hurt bad than a little stiffenin' of the blood, a little liftin' of the spirit, and a relaxin' of the mind."

Amilie gazed after him until the pain in her broken arm drove her to a chair. She didn't sit long; that kicking horse down in the barn was going to make slivers out of the door if someone didn't turn him loose so he could find water. She dragged herself down there, making a point of not looking aside or downward as she left the porch.

The broken arm throbbed, felt feverish but did not hurt as much now as it had when the break occurred. She turned the horse loose. It went out the rear of the barn like a cannonball as Amilie walked up front, sat down on a little wooden keg, and leaned forward, feeling faint for the first time since all hell had busted loose in the yard. Faintness could have been caused by her injury, or her exhaustion, or perhaps even because she had killed a man, but actually what bowed her spirit was the full expectation that Ashe Colby would die.

He'd bled in the dirt of the yard and had still been bleeding when they'd got him onto a bed in the house. Not as heavily as Henry Knight had bled, but for a longer period of time.

She forced herself to get up and start walking. That grimy, sweaty man would need hot water. When she paused for seconds on the porch, listening to Elizabeth's muffled sobs as she held Samuel to her, the full impact of what had happened struck her, hard.

The people with whom she had lived since childhood were dead except for Elizabeth, and perhaps old Sidney. She wouldn't know about him for some time yet, but as far as Amilie was concerned, if he was indeed dead she would not shed a single tear.

Hoskins was bellowing from the back of the house. Amilie filled a pot with hot water at the stove, ground her teeth against the pain of carrying it, and went down the dingy hallway to Sidney's bedroom. Everything had been ransacked as though the cache-hunters hadn't believed all his cache was atop the kitchen table.

Hoskins was working with rolled-up sleeves. He glared at her. "Pull that little table up close. Where the hell's the basin, girl?"

She went stolidly back to the kitchen and returned with a basin, which she put on the little bedside table. Hoskins straightened and scowled at her. The older man on the bed was unconscious with blood still leaking, but only in drops now. His exposed body was beginning to swell and become discolored. Hoskins said, "Go lie down, girl. Take a jolt from this jug an' go lie down before you faint plumb away. I said take a jolt from that damned jug. You take it or I'll set on you an' pour it down you. *Take it!*"

Those last two words had the whiplash sound of a voice belonging to a man whose exasperation has reached its limit.

Amilie had trouble hoisting the jug, so Hoskins spared her a moment to help. She swallowed, gagged, and bent over as he put the jug aside and slapped her a couple of times on the back. "Now go lie down. *Go!*"

She was in the doorway with her back to the room when a very tired voice half whispered from the bed, "Cranky ol' bastard."

Hoskins's entire demeanor changed. All signs of anxiety and weariness left his face. "I thought you was passed out."

"I was until you yelled at the girl. What time of day is it?"

"Close to evening. Don't talk, Henry. You lost a lot of blood."

"You don't say? How'd you ever figure that out?"

When Hoskins started to reply, Knight went limp from head to toes.

Hoskins held his breath, watching for trickles of blood. If they failed to appear it would mean Knight's heart had stopped pumping. It was the longest short wait of Ace Hoskins's entire life.

Blood oozed around a soggy, big absorbent bandage. Hoskins looked for the jug, had two swallows for himself, and went to work with hot water and more clean rags.

He had to stop once to light a lamp, which he placed on the little bedside table. He turned with a back that ached from leaning over the bed so long, washed his hands in the basin, and looked for a long time at the lifeless-appearing face in poor lamplight.

Voices in another part of the house brought him around toward the dingy hallway. He went searching for their source.

Elizabeth and Amilie were in Ashe Colby's room. When Hoskins appeared in the doorway, their backs were to him as Amilie said, "Yes, I'll help you," and the older woman, round-shouldered from exhaustion and dull-voiced, protested. "No. You stay with this one. I'll do it." She turned and saw Hoskins standing there. For seconds the suffering in her eyes was replaced by a hostile look, then she brushed past and went toward another part of the house. Hoskins looked after her as he spoke to Amilie. "She seems all right."

Amilie, who had been bathing Colby and tending his injuries, replied softly. "She isn't. She's—something has happened to her mind. She wanted me to help her take some blankets to the porch so she could make Sam'l comfortable while he slept." Amilie turned. "He's dead."

Hoskins gazed at the girl's puffy face and swollen mouth. Nothing he could say would have any bearing on Samuel Rigdon, so he reminded her he'd told her to rest. She turned her back to him and resumed her one-armed care of Ashe Colby.

Without moving from the doorway, Hoskins asked about

the wounds. Amilie's answer was perfunctory. "One hit that big buckle on his shell-belt and knocked the air out of him. Come over here near the lamp and you can see."

Hoskins still remained in the doorway. "That's all?"

"No. But that's the one that bled the most. The other one is between his ribs and his arm. It cut him in both places."

Hoskins nodded. "Pretty close," he murmured. Amilie said nothing as she worked, but Ashe Colby did. He said, "How's Henry?"

Finally, Hoskins approached the bed; he had not wanted to go over there and look at the face of another friend who might die. But Colby had been washed and bandaged. He looked gaunt and pale but clear-eyed as Hoskins smiled at him. "Henry's hangin' on, but he bled like a stuck hog."

Colby considered the older man's face. "You look like hell," he said, and smiled a little.

Hoskins smiled back. "Strange you should say that, because I feel like hell."

Amilie straightened up, looked for something to sit on, and fainted. Hoskins caught her crumbling form, lifted her as though she were a child as Colby said, "Put her here beside me."

Hoskins declined. "I'll take her out to the parlor an' get that arm splinted before she wakes up. Maybe."

"She won't stay out that long, Ace."

Hoskins turned without another word and carried the girl to a battered old horsehide sofa, went after the lamp he'd used in Knight's room, paused a moment to lean down and listen to his friend's breathing, then returned to the parlor.

Elizabeth was standing there, perfectly erect with both hands clasped in front of her. Without looking at Hoskins, she asked if Amilie was hurt.

He gave her a puzzled look when he replied. "Yeah. I need some slats and some cloth to set her busted arm."

Elizabeth turned, still without looking at the man, and went out to the kitchen.

Hoskins got the arm straightened with one eye watching Amilie's face. He sliced the sleeve to the shoulder with his clasp knife, and when Elizabeth returned, looking and acting perfectly normal, to hand him some clean sacking and two smooth pieces from the kindling box, he looked at her. She would not meet his gaze and took the same stance she'd had before, erect, expressionless, hands clasped over her stomach.

Hoskins sighed and went to work. When he said, "How's your boy?" Elizabeth replied matter-of-factly, "The bleeding stopped. He's sleeping now."

Hoskins said, "Good. Now then, if you'll hold her wrist while I pull from above, we can get the bones to mesh."

Elizabeth obediently gripped the girl's wrist in both hands, stared at Amilie's face and not at Hoskins as he exerted gradual pressure, but she said, "Do you know what you're doing?"

"I've set bones before. Now then, keep that pressure, I want to feel the bone."

". . . Is it all right?"

"Yes'm. Now keep the pressure on an' pray she don't wake up while I set the splints and bandage the arm."

Elizabeth's eyes did not leave the girl's face. "She won't wake up. Amilie's a good girl."

Hoskins neither looked at the woman nor said anything until he'd completed setting and wrapping the arm, then, as before in Knight's room, he had to straighten up slowly because of back pain. He grimaced as he said, "Ease up now. When she comes around, help her shove it back inside her shirt."

Elizabeth eased up, folded both hands again, and stood like a statue, a gaunt, hard-featured woman of indeterminate years with a stone-set to her thin lips and eyes that seemed to reflect something from inside her soul that was shielding her from the worst thing that could have happened to her, and which had happened.

Hoskins stood hip-shot watching Amilie breathe. "She ought to come around, hadn't she?" he muttered more to himself than to the woman.

Elizabeth's gaze went swiftly to his profile, then fled back to the girl on the old sofa. "She'll come around. Thank your lucky stars she didn't do it when you was pullin' on those bones. Her face looks awful. What happened to her?"

Hoskins stood looking at the girl as he said, "You'll have to ask her. I got to get back to Henry."

Elizabeth stopped him near the dark hallway, still with her back to him. "I'll fix something to eat. Can your friend sit up?"

"No, ma'am, an' he can't eat either."

She still refused to look at him. "Nonsense. He has to eat."

Hoskins continued on his way, and when he entered the bedroom, which was now faintly lighted by weak moonlight and starshine, he faltered. Knight hadn't moved.

He crossed to the side of the bed, leaned down and listened for a heartbeat, heard nothing, and pushed his ear harder against Knight's chest.

There was a beat, slow and sluggish but faintly steady. Hoskins pulled up a chair and sat down. Within two minutes he was asleep, head on his chest, body sprawled, legs pushed straight out.

He heard nothing and saw nothing when the dark wraith arrived, stopped to consider both men, then stepped to the side of the bed, got an arm beneath Knight's head and hoisted him up a little, got the rim of a thick crockery mug to his mouth, and with all the patience in the world worked the mug very slowly, not forcing Henry to swallow but trickling the cup's contents into his throat, which automatically opened and closed.

After the wraith had departed Hoskins was awakened by Knight making puppylike sounds in his throat. Hoskins stood up in dread. He'd heard death rattles before.

Hoskins stopped making the sounds, his breathing re-

sumed and his partner stood frowning in puzzlement as
Hoskins breathed a little sigh.

Elizabeth appeared in the doorway, hands clasped. Hoskins looked around irritably. "Lady, I told you, he can't eat."

Elizabeth accepted the rebuke as though she had not
understood it to be one. She said, "There's hot food in the
kitchen. You better come."

When Ace Hoskins eased back down on the chair and eyed
the whiskey jug, Elizabeth spoke again in the same matter-
of-fact, short way. "What you need isn't in that jug, mister.
You come along with me. Right now before everything gets
cold."

He turned to look at her. "How's the girl?"

"Still sleeping."

Elizabeth filled the doorway like an avenging angel. Hoskins blew out a breath, pushed up off the chair, and Elizabeth turned to lead the way to the lighted kitchen where she
had prepared a large meal. She had also made hot beef
broth, but Hoskins wasn't interested in that as he sank down
at the table and speared a hefty steak.

Elizabeth watched him briefly then said, "I'll go see if Sam'l
is still asleep, then I'll come back an' maybe Amilie'll be
awake by then. She needs food. She never did put on no
weight where she's supposed to."

Hoskins did not look up as the gaunt woman marched out
of the kitchen, but as she was crossing the parlor he twisted
on the chair to look after her, wearing a troubled expression.

CHAPTER 19

Another Day

WHEN Elizabeth returned, Hoskins was finishing his meal. When he asked how her son was, she got busy at the stove before replying. "Still sleeping. He's pretty tucked up. The last few days taken a lot out of him. Sam'l's a good boy. If it'd been just him an' me, he'd have got along fine."

Hoskins got to his feet. No one had taken care of her horse. He went out to the porch and looked at Samuel, whose body had been tenderly covered with a blanket and whose face had been washed. Then he went to do the chores.

Those saddled horses were behind the barn as though expecting someone to unsaddle them. Hoskins did that too. He pitched out some feed, stalled the dapple gray, and walked up front to stand in the cooling night where stars like brilliant grains of sand were everywhere, listening for sounds. Any kind, but particularly the sound of mounted men and wagons. All he heard was the mournful call of a night bird. Behind him something made a furtive sound that brought Hoskins wide awake as he swung to face whatever it was, six-gun in his fist, thumb atop the hammer.

A large barn owl disappeared through the rear opening.

Hoskins holstered the weapon, looked toward the lighted house, and with no enthusiasm at all went over to drag dead men away by the ankles. When he paused with the last one to rest, Amilie appeared on the porch. She said, "I'll help you."

He looked irritably at the arm inside her shirt when he

replied. "You won't do any such a thing. This is man's work. You go look in on Colby an' my partner."

"I already did." She seemed to be softly smiling, but it was difficult to be certain because the porch's warped old overhang had her imprisoned in darkness. "Your partner took more broth from Elizabeth. She washed his face and he smiled at her just before he went back to sleep."

Hoskins let the dead man's legs drop.

"And Ashe said he wanted to get up."

"Did you let him—the damned fool?"

"No, Mister Hoskins. He couldn't do it."

"Give him a jolt from that jug an' I'll be along directly. . . . Girl? How do you feel?"

She had eaten and had sipped a cupful of Elizabeth Rigdon's cure-all, hot beef broth. "Better than I've felt in days. Mister Hoskins; thank you for setting my arm."

He squinted at her. "How did it get broke?"

"The man you shot between the eyes; that was Sam'l's brother. I never liked him an' he never liked me. When they got inside the house I heard 'em and got the shotgun. They came into the parlor an' stopped dead still when I cocked it. Joseph told me to put it down."

"What did you do?"

"Pulled one trigger, then the other trigger. It wasn't loaded, Mister Hoskins. He grabbed the gun, swung it like a club, and when I threw up my arm to protect my head, the barrels broke my arm. I screamed. He grabbed me and struck me with his fists until Sam'l pulled him off."

Hoskins's gaze drifted to the "sleeping" man behind her on the porch. He sighed and repeated what he'd told her before. "Go look after Henry an' Ashe. I'll be along directly."

She nodded and went back into the house.

The last corpse he dragged to the shelter of the barn was that of Joseph Rigdon. After Hoskins had him inside, out of the runway, he stood a moment eyeing what was eerily visible by feeble light, spat, and returned to the yard. Everybody died and some folks deserved to die, but that son of a bitch back there should have died a couple more times before he finally did.

He was feeling better but very tired as he trudged back to the porch. Samuel was lying exactly as he had been since before nightfall, on his side with his face to one side, eyes closed, a serene expression on his face. Hoskins said, "Sorry," and entered the house where lamplight made him blink.

Amilie and Elizabeth were in the kitchen. He passed on through to Knight's room first, where his partner was making noises like a shoat caught under a gate, and that was reassuring, for while Hoskins had complained many times, loudly and vehemently, about Henry Knight's snoring, standing at bedside this particular night the sound was like music.

He went down the opposite hall to Colby's room and interrupted a hand-holding moment when Colby looked over the girl's shoulder and saw him in the doorway. He asked how Knight was, and Amilie yanked her hand free, got off the side of the bed, and avoided Hoskins's gaze as she slipped past him.

He went over to the bedside, looked for something to sit on, found a three-cornered stool, and perched on it as he said, "He's snoring. I guess that's a good sign. But damned if I know why it should be, he lost enough blood to drown a horse. How about you?"

Colby reached to roll down his covers. "You want to see?"

Hoskins replied swiftly. "No. I just asked."

"His first slug would've gone through me from front to back except for that big shell-belt buckle. It drove the buckle into my belly, carved up some hide and meat, made it impossible for me to breathe for a spell. I thought sure as hell he'd killed me."

Hoskins jutted his jaw. "That's where the other one went—between your upper arm and your side?"

"Yeah. Tore some meat an' bled a lot, but I've been hurt

worse an' didn't even stop talking. But my belly's sore as a boil."

Hoskins raised a hand to scratch his cheek. He already knew most of what he'd been told and he was tired of hearing about such things anyway. "Cap should have showed up by now," he said, and Colby shook his head. "Not if he's got those wagons with him. They were packin' heavy loads. Tomorrow he'll get down here."

Hoskins eyed the younger man impassively before saying, "That's a tough girl." He paused and glanced elsewhere while clearing his throat. "An' she's got to be older'n she looks."

Colby waited, watching the other man's face.

"But she don't look like a woman. How old is she, anyway, fourteen?"

"Crowding nineteen," replied Colby, and was not at all surprised at the look of incredulity that settled on Hoskins's face as the older man stared at Colby and said, "Nineteen? Partner, I've seen fat boys got more—"

"Mister Hoskins, I know what you're goin' to say an' the first time I saw her I thought the same thing, but partner, she's got more grit in her craw than half the men in the territory."

Hoskins sat on the stool gazing at his hands. "Built like a boy," he grumbled. "An' a pretty young one at that. Naw, she can't be nineteen, Ashe."

"I said she's *crowding* nineteen. She's eighteen." As Colby said this he put a chilly gaze upon the older man. "Mister Hoskins, if what you're thinkin' is so important, I expect when you get married you'd better find a holstein cow. They got four of 'em, an' they're big."

Elizabeth appeared in the doorway, prim and erect. "Amilie thought she saw a rider far out."

Both men looked at her. "Which direction?" Hoskins asked, arising from the little stool.

"From the east."

Hoskins turned slowly to exchange a look with Ashe Colby; when he turned back the gaunt woman was gone. Hoskins went as far as the door before turning to speak. "If they had a fight up north an' are on their way down here, wouldn't they be comin' from the north instead of the east?"

Colby thought so. "Seems likely. Mister Hoskins, be careful."

The morning was still young, the heat that would arrive before high noon was still some hours off as Hoskins went after his carbine in the barn and reloaded it from among the weapons the dead men had owned.

He remained in the barn where he could see for many miles but where indoor gloom camouflaged him very well. Amilie came in from out back, also with a saddlegun, which she carried in one hand. Hoskins turned, rolled his eyes, and wordlessly faced forward again.

She walked up closer. "He's not out there now, but he was."

"You sure, girl? I don't see anything."

She raised the carbine to use as a pointer as she said, "There. Hard to see him with the sun at his back. You see him?"

Not for a few moments he didn't, and even when he finally made out the moving shape it was so distant he scowled in her direction. If she'd spotted him fifteen minutes earlier when he'd been even farther off, she had the eyes of an eagle. His gaze dropped a little, then raised again. Maybe the Good Lord had compensated for what he hadn't given her much of by giving her other things, such as extraordinary eyesight, a steady gunhand, and that toughness he'd mentioned earlier.

In this country and under present circumstances, those things were more important anyway. He sank to one knee and leaned on his appropriated Winchester, squinting hard so as not to lose sight of the oncoming horseman.

Amilie remained upright. She said, "He's sure as hell in no hurry, is he?"

Hoskins looked a little startled. Of course women were as entitled to swear as men were, it was just that so few had ever done it in his presence that it startled him whenever one did, especially such a young one. And especially when they did it so casually.

The rider was adequately visible when he halted out there in the sun-bright open grassland, made no move toward any of the jumbles of gray rock that would have concealed him, and sat like a carving looking in the direction of the yard.

Amilie said, "Scout."

Hoskins nodded but said nothing as the rider eased forward to begin moving again. "Could be an In'ian," he said.

Amilie contradicted him. "No. It's a white man."

Hoskins got a little red in the face. "Is he now?"

"Yes, an' he's got a carbine on the left side, butt-up."

Hoskins got sarcastic. "An' what color's the horse, girl?"

"Liver chestnut."

Hoskins froze for three seconds. "Are you plumb sure of that? It looks black to me."

"I'm sure," she told him, and finally sank down beside him to also lean on her gun, but with only one hand holding it.

Hoskins sighed. He could make out the man atop the horse but not a gun sticking up on the left side, and not the color of the horse, but both of those things had significance to him. One might not have; the gun on the left side, for instance. Lots of men were left-handed. But of all the colors horses came in, liver chestnut was probably the rarest. Certainly there was no other such horse among the men he'd ridden up here from Rosalia with, except the one he was looking at.

He was still straining to see far out when he asked Amilie a question. "Big man?"

She said, "Big and heavy with his hat pulled real low in front."

Hoskins got stiffly upright. "Whiskers, girl?"

"No whiskers, Mister Hoskins."

He looked down at her. "Go up to the house an' tell Ashe Cap's coming."

She dutifully stood up, still looking out there. "You know him?"

"If your description is right I know him. So does Ashe."

She turned to face the older man. "Who is he?"

"The head Ranger; feller named Captain Frank Hauser."

"What's he doing out there by himself? Where are the men Ashe an' you said would be coming with him?"

"Well now, girl, if I knew all that, I wouldn't have to wonder about it myself, would I? Go tell Ashe. He's lyin' in there fretting."

She smiled at Hoskins. "You don't make it easy for a person to like you. But I like you anyway."

He twisted to watch her leave the barn the same way she'd entered it, by the rear doorway, and shortly before she passed from sight he told himself that from the rear she sure enough looked like a female woman.

She had long, thick, wavy hair.

CHAPTER 20

"After the Race Has Been Run"

THAT liver chestnut horse was big. Amilie guessed he weighed about eleven hundred pounds. In a reining competition he'd have lost to everything but mules. But he had to be big: his rider swung off out in front of the barn where Ace Hoskins walked out to greet him, and with his back to the house, with Hoskins in front of the stranger, she couldn't see Hoskins at all.

Because of his breadth, the man did not appear to be tall, but he was. He was dusty, sweat-stained, and rumpled-looking. Amilie told Elizabeth if all Rangers were as large as this one they wouldn't need more than one or two to each battle.

Elizabeth, who had been busy in the kitchen since sunup, neither went to look nor commented. She may not even have heard the girl. Elizabeth was cooking, boiling water, stirring, baking, moving efficiently and endlessly from stove to cupboards to sink to table and back to the stove. She hadn't spoken since she'd appeared in Colby's doorway to announce the appearance of that big man talking to Ace Hoskins down at the barn.

They moved inside the barn where the big man cared for his horse and continued their palaver in there. The big man stood above the corpses, looking at each one with individual attention. He had a memory for faces on reward dodgers, but whether any of the dead men fit those descriptions or pictures he did not say as he turned back toward Hoskins.

"One of the wagons'll have to turn off an' come over here for Henry an' Ashe."

Hoskins did not contradict the large man with the uncompromising jaw and testy gaze, he simply made a suggestion. "There's a rig in the equipment shed an' there's a horse somewhere around here that'll pull it. Won't waste any time that way, Cap."

The big man gazed past Hoskins out into the sunshine. "All right. I'd as soon not have to wait."

"Are they behind you?"

The testy eyes returned to Hoskins's face. "Not that we know of an' we been keepin' a sharp watch up the back-trail. But we got quite a herd of prisoners, an' they sure as hell got kinfolk and friends who'll want them freed."

"By any chance you got one named Sidney Rigdon?"

The big man walked up front to lean in the doorway, looking around the yard as he said, "Yes, we got the old son of a bitch. An' another of their elders, feller named Porter Hanson." Satisfied with what he'd seen of the yard, he gazed at the front of the house to the limp form on the porch as he said, "That's the one you told me about, under those blankets near the door?"

"Yes. Samuel Rigdon. Big enough to eat hay an' born with one foot out of the stirrup an' been like that ever since."

Captain Hauser spat, reset his hat in his favorite position, well down to shade his eyes, and said, "Let's go see Henry an' Ashe."

By the time they were nearing the long, wide porch steps, Amilie had seen them coming and told Elizabeth, who neither looked at the girl nor spoke, but got busy setting the table and going back and forth between it and the stove for platters of food, moving briskly, keeping busy.

When the two men crossed the parlor to the kitchen door,

Amilie was no longer there; she'd gone to Colby's room to tell him about the big man.

Elizabeth raised a hand to push back a straggling length of graying hair and looked the big man straight in the eye as she said, "Set down, it's ready."

To Hoskins's astonishment, Captain Hauser tossed his hat in a corner, sat down, pulled a faded old blue bandana from a pocket, and tucked it neatly into his collar. Without speaking or looking at the gaunt woman, he loaded his platter and started to eat.

The silence was total except for the big man, whose knife and fork made busy, small sounds. Hoskins was uncomfortable. He turned on tiptoes and left the big man and the gaunt woman alone in the kitchen.

She refilled Hauser's cup with coffee twice, then rolled her eyes in exasperation, got the whiskey jug, and set it on the table as she said, "You'll ruin perfectly good coffee."

Captain Hauser, who was not much of a drinking man and who was adamant about himself or any of his men drinking while they were on a trail, did not even grunt. He ignored Elizabeth, tipped in a splash of whiskey, shoved the jug back, and raised the cup.

Their eyes met as he drank. Elizabeth turned away and became busy at the stove as she said, "When you come stampin' in you didn't wake my boy on the porch, did you?"

Frank Hauser put the cup down. "No, ma'am."

"I'm beholden. These other men don't care. 'Specially that one who come in with you."

Hauser resumed his meal. He required a lot of sustenance and Elizabeth had supplied it. Later, as he was arising and pulling down the faded bandana, he studied her for a long moment before saying, "You're a whale of a cook, Miz Rigdon. Person like you don't belong in this godforsaken country."

Elizabeth did not turn to look at him or to speak.

He drained the coffee cup and walked massively from the

room. Hoskins was waiting over in the gloomy hallway. He said, "You see what I mean about her?"

Captain Hauser's brooding, pale eyes looked down the hallway. "Who's back there?"

Hoskins led the way, and when the big man moved up to Knight's bedside his voice was surprisingly soft for a man of his heft. "You old screwt, are you goin' to just lie there when there's work to be done?"

Knight's eyes opened slowly, drowsily. A hint of a smile shadowed his chapped, beard-stubbled lips. "You done it again, Cap. Showed up when all the fun's over."

"How do you feel? You sure look like hell."

The very tired-appearing eyes moved slowly up and down before Henry spoke again. "Remember that girl down at—"

"I asked how you feel, Henry!"

"Wasn't she about the prettiest thing you ever set your eyes on, Cap?"

The big man grudgingly inclined his head. "Yes, she was."

". . . How do I feel? Like I been dragged through a knothole an' stamped on."

"Go to sleep."

Knight obeyed. In fact, he was asleep before the big man and Hoskins had reached the parlor on their way to the other sickroom. Frank Hauser stopped Hoskins in the parlor and shook his head. Hoskins did not seem to notice as he resumed his way and stood back for Captain Hauser to enter Colby's room, where Amilie was sitting ramrod straight in a chair.

He saw the girl and ignored her to stop beside Colby's bed, looking down. Colby smiled. "Good to see you."

Hauser nodded gravely. "Good to see you, boy. We got a feller named Hanson. He told us he'd caught you up near where we overtook the wagons. You—an' someone else."

Colby saw Hoskins standing slightly behind Hauser and to one side. Hoskins looked uncomfortable, particularly so when Colby's smile faded before he spoke.

"That's her sitting yonder. Amilie Prescott. She can shoot straight an' ride like an' In'ian. Amilie, this is Captain Hauser."

They looked at each other. Amilie would have smiled if the big man had, but he didn't, he barely inclined his head to her then returned his attention to Ashe Colby. "How bad are you hurt?"

Colby explained about the bullet striking his shell-belt buckle. He didn't have to explain where else he'd been shot. The bandages were very visible, and during his explanation the big man's gaze suggested that he was only half listening; he was making a judgment about the chances for Colby's recovery. Evidently he thought they were excellent, because he fished in a pocket, brought forth a cheroot and lit it, let smoke trickle, and told Colby about what he'd said to Hoskins down at the barn.

"We got the wagons and a herd of prisoners. They're over on the stage road goin' south. Ace'll put you boys in a buggy over here an' catch up with us." Hauser paused to look at the ash on his cigar. "We got two men hurt a little an' we lined up the other ones, the fellers who got killed last night; left 'em up there in a neat row so's when they're found their friends an' kinsmen can look after 'em." Hauser paused again, this time to tip ash into a little plate on the bedside table.

"Couple of the prisoners aren't in very good shape." There was not a sound in the room as the others stared, and waited. "Feller named Hanson got hit pretty hard in the side, an' Rosalia's a hell of a distance for a man in his shape. The other prisoners told me there's no doctor in this country, unless we want to go north ninety miles, an' hell, Rosalia's closer."

Colby said, "Rigdon?"

Captain Hauser rolled the stogie in his mouth before answering. He could be sarcastic when something inclined him to be that way. "Well, Mister Rigdon's somethin' you don't run across too often. He never fired a shot, an' when it was over we had to climb into the wagon and drag him out from behind all that iron an' those boxes full of spankin'-new counterfeit money. He was real cooperative; told us about a cache down here he'd trade us for a horse an' a half-hour head start. Yes sir, he's the sort of feller who makes a real fine hero."

Colby had a question. "Did you run across a feller named Jethro and a couple called called Don and Jack?"

Captain Hauser nodded. "Yes, that's when we heard about the young lady here. By the way, that McKenna feller had a reward on him down in Texas. Killed a lawman in a town down there."

Amilie arose and stole from the room as silent as a mouse. The big man turned as she disappeared beyond the door, exchanged a glance with Ace Hoskins, and removed the cigar to gaze at it as he said, "You got to give the devil his due, but I still don't like you boys gettin' involved with females when you're on a trail."

Colby's mouth was pulled flat. Hoskins saw this and fidgeted. He knew from experience that Captain Hauser was an uncompromising lawman. No one crossed him and walked away without at least smarting.

Colby said, "I'll draw my pay when we get back to Rosalia."

The big man's pale eyes rose slowly to Colby's face. "Why? Because of her?"

"Maybe, but mostly because I'd have been dead a couple of times except for her, an' I don't want to work for a man who treated her like you just did."

Hauser leaned to put his dead stogie in the little dish. Then he walked out to the porch. There he stood looking northward, hat low in front, hands in his trouser pockets. Elizabeth appeared soundlessly to loosen the blankets over Samuel. Hauser turned to watch. When she made a little crooning sound, he continued to watch until she was straightening up, then he softly said, "He'll be better with those covers down a little. It's gettin' hot."

Elizabeth remained a long moment with her back to the big man, then turned very slowly. "Yes. Directly it'll be even hotter."

He nodded solemnly about that, eyes on Samuel. "I'll carry him inside if it gets too hot."

"You don't have to, Mister Hauser."

His pale eyes went up to her face. "Be glad to, Missus Rigdon. If you got a minute I'd like to tell you a story."

She did not say whether she had a minute or not. In fact, she didn't say anything as she stood facing him, work-roughened hands clasped in front.

"When I was eighteen Satanta's Kiowas made a horse raid through our part of west Texas. That was after they turned him loose after serving only two years of a life sentence to prison for other raids.

"I was in the root cellar an' didn't even know they was attacking until I heard my mother and younger brother screamin' over at the house. My paw was shot dead in the doorway when he stepped out to see what the commotion was about at the corrals.

"My brother was twelve years old. He ran to Paw, picked up the rifle, an' a buck killed him before he could cock it. They took all our horses and by the time I got over to the house, they were a mile off, ridin' hard.

"We buried Paw that night, but Maw had my brother in his bed covered like he was sleeping."

Elizabeth interrupted. "You said he was killed in the doorway."

Captain Hauser nodded at her. "He was, ma'am."

The big man and the gaunt, worn woman stood silently facing each other for a long time. Amilie saw them like that beyond the broken window. She had heard Hauser talking, had listened to everything he'd said, and had to sit down.

Elizabeth's mouth quivered, otherwise she remained erect and unyielding.

Captain Hauser's eyes did not leave her face. "Missus Rigdon . . . ?"

Elizabeth's eyes blurred, her hands were so tightly clenched against her stomach the knuckles shone white, but she refused to allow her body to relax.

The big man with the iron jaw and cold blue eyes startled Amilie. He walked over, gently took Elizabeth in his massive arms, and held her tenderly.

She finally yielded. Sobs shook her whole body, tears dripped on his rough shirt, she opened and closed her hands against his chest. He stood silently as the choking sobs in her throat finally broke past her lips in a series of wails.

Hoskins came hurriedly from the back of the house, saw Amilie sitting there expressionless and soundless with tears running down both cheeks, looked out the window, and unconsciously widened his eyes to their limits.

Hoskins tiptoed back the way he had come.

Elizabeth's grief seemed endless once the dams broke. Colby heard her and fretfully plucked at his covers in an effort to leave the bed. Amilie appeared in the doorway tear-streaked and anguished. She went over, pushed gently against his chest, and shook her head.

He asked her what was happening. All she could do was continue to shake her head, ease down on the side of the bed, and bury her head against him.

Captain Hauser seemed prepared to stand out there holding Elizabeth for as long as it was required of him, and it was indeed a long time before she hung limply in his arms, the sobs diminishing, the violent tremors decreasing in frequency and violence.

He helped her down off the porch as though she were an invalid, held her by the hand and walked slowly with her in a direction the sun could not reach either of their faces, and gauged his stride to her shorter one as he kept her moving.

Out where they stopped, their backs were to the buildings, the yard, the off-center sun. He said, "Before I left home for the last time, I wrote a little poem for my mother. Would you like to hear it, Missus Rigdon?"

Elizabeth's reply was a whisper. "Yes."

"After the loving is over,
After the race has been run,
After the tears and the heartache,
You still have a place in the sun."

CHAPTER 21

An Interruption

WHEN Colby heard the whole story from Ace Hoskins, who had watched them leave the porch, he lay back staring at the ceiling. Amilie brought him hot broth, which he drank, smiling tenderly at her but saying nothing until she spoke.

"It's awful how wrong folks can be. I took an instant dislike to him from the moment he came inside." She perched on the edge of the bed. "Do you know him very well?"

Colby looked rueful. "I thought I did. I been workin' under him for a long time. I've ridden out with him, but maybe I never really did, Amilie. I told him I was quitting over the way he treated you."

She leaned to gently stroke his cheek with a cool palm. "Don't do it, Ashe. Not over me anyway." She pulled the hand back. "If I live to be a hundred I don't expect to ever see another man as gentle as he was with Elizabeth. It made me cry. Do you know what he did? You nor I couldn't have done it. He didn't tell her Sam'l was dead, but somehow he knew she knew it, so he told her a story about his little brother bein' killed and his mother actin' toward him the way Elizabeth's been acting about Sam'l. Ashe, I'll never forget him."

"Where are they now?"

She had no idea. "Around somewhere. He held her for near a half hour until all the heartache was spent out of her. I didn't know a man could have that much understanding." Amilie got off the bed and picked up the empty broth cup.

171

"I'll get you some more." From the doorway, she said, "That's the first time I ever saw a man like him."

Colby was lying motionless, watching a fragile spider at work in a corner of the wall up near the ceiling when Captain Hauser walked in with the cup of broth. Colby looked from the cup to the granite face of the big man. Hauser held out the cup. "Met the girl in the parlor. She asked me to take this to you. Sure smells good. There's nothin' like hot beef broth to put a person on the mend."

Colby held the cup. "I didn't mean what I said, Cap. About quittin' anyway, but I meant the rest of it."

Hauser eased his massive frame down upon the chair Amilie had used earlier. He considered ham-sized hands as he spoke. "I was hopin' you didn't, boy. As for the girl . . ."

"What about her?"

"Her an' Miz Rigdon can't stay here. Well, Miz Rigdon could, but it wouldn't be good for her. Maybe when you'n Henry'n Ace leave, you'd better take that old wagon in the shed. It'll be big enough." Hauser stopped examining his hands. "Those folks will find the bodies in the barn. When this place is empty an' abandoned, they'll sneak in here like wolves."

Colby was beginning to frown faintly. Frank Hauser was making a lot of disjointed conversation.

The big man smiled slightly. "I got no idea what we'll do with them."

"The folks who'll sneak in here after we're gone?"

"No. The girl and Miz Rigdon."

"You said we'd take 'em along in the wagon."

"I didn't mean that, boy. I meant what'll we do with them when we get back to Rosalia? The girl'll make out. She's young and resourceful, but Miz Rigdon's spent most of her life up here. She don't know anythin' else and everything she knows—and knew—is up here."

Hauser got to his feet. "An' I got another problem. She wants to bury her youngest out back beneath an old cottonwood tree. You can't help, neither can Henry. Ace could, an' so could I, except that I told the lads that I'd meet them down-country today some time."

Colby felt the cup cooling in his hands so he drained it, put it aside, and considered the big man with the granite jaw and gray-steel eyes. Hauser walked out of the room without another word or glance.

Someone in the parlor called sharply to someone else. Hoskins appeared in Colby's doorway carrying a Winchester. "Company coming," he said, and turned abruptly away, leaving Colby full of wonder and worry.

The sun was fairly well up there by now, so there was a little heat in the new day, not enough to cause that blue-blur which would arrive later but enough faint shimmering to make the distant riders appear to be traveling six or eight inches above the ground as their shapes changed with the blur of distance.

Hoskins leaned near the broken window, looking out as he spoke to the big man. "Five of 'em."

Back in the shadows Amilie corrected him. "Four, Mister Hoskins."

He turned, scowling irritably. "Who are they?" he asked, making it sound like a challenge.

She replied as she moved slightly closer to the window. "That man out front is Elder Jensen. Behind him is—"

"Counterfeiters?" asked Captain Hauser, without taking his eyes off the approaching riders.

"No. Elder Jensen's a spiritual man. He's been a comfort to me a few times. You know anythin' about Navajo Indians, Captain?"

"Why do you ask?"

"Because if you do, why then you know they got medicine men called Roadmen. They travel all the time, goin' from camp to camp treatin' the sick, doin' their rituals, marryin' an' burying."

"Are you talking about that feller out there, Jensen?"

"Yes."

Hauser went closer to the window, stood with hands behind his back for a while, then said, "I'm goin' down to the barn, Ace. Maybe they're peaceful an' maybe they aren't, an' if they aren't, when they ride past the barn I'll be behind 'em. You stay in the house."

The riders were not approaching the yard in any kind of haste. They were riding bunched up though, and probably silent as they studied the yard.

The place looked deserted. There were no horses out back, no sign of life at the house, no one came forth to meet them.

The man in front stopped, rested both hands atop the saddlehorn; the leggy, speckled roan horse he was astride hung its head as though there were no interesting scents coming out to him. None of the other horses evinced any more interest, and that encouraged the two men and two women to push ahead, still at a cautious walk.

Hoskins asked Amilie a question without taking his eyes off the newcomers. "You know them all?"

Elizabeth answered from near the kitchen door. "Elder Jensen's on that savinna-lookin' horse. That woman on his right an' back a tad is his wife."

"The tall woman on the bay horse?"

"Yes. An' the man behind Elder Jensen is Arlie Cobb. That's his wife beside him. Mister Cobb's a deacon."

Hoskins gazed over at Elizabeth but said nothing. She ignored his glance and moved slightly closer to the middle of the room where she could see the yard better. She was watching the front barn opening, but she seemed to be watching the riders who were now entering the yard.

Hoskins asked Elizabeth a question, since she seemed so knowledgeable. "What do they want? How did they happen to show up down here?"

Elizabeth was removing her apron when she replied. "They'll know what's been happening. Word spreads faster'n fire in this country, Mister Hoskins. I'll go see what they want."

"No, ma'am. You stay right where you are!"

The four riders stopped at the barn tie-rack and dismounted. As far as Hoskins could see, they had no weapons. At least there were no saddleguns or short-guns showing.

The man Amilie had identified as Jensen leaned on the off-side of his horse, gazing in the direction of the house across his saddle-seat. Hoskins wagged his head a little. People who kept a horse between themselves and a house while they studied things out hadn't always been preachers, or whatever he was.

The shorter, more husky of the two women gave a little squeal. Both men turned. Captain Hauser was in the doorway, a carbine held loosely in both hands as he said, "Good mornin', folks."

The newcomers stared at him. The shorter man named Cobb looked very uncomfortable as he said, "Good morning. Mind tellin' us who you are?"

"Frank Hauser—Captain, Arizona Rangers. Mind tellin' me who you folks are an' what you want here?"

Cobb mopped sweat with a huge red bandana as he replied. "This here is Elder Jensen. That tall lady is his wife. Me, I'm Deacon Cobb, an' this here is my wife."

Frank Hauser nodded gravely. "Glad to meet you folks. Now then, what do you want here?"

Elder Jensen, who was as tall as Captain Hauser and clearly a muscular man although carrying a little paunch, spoke quietly while looking straight at Frank Hauser. "We came down from St. George four days back in response to rumors of trouble down here. Six of our company stayed up where we found some dead men lined out. They're to bury them, then follow our tracks." Elder Jensen gestured in the direction of the house. "Is that a dead man under that blanket on the porch, Captain Hauser?"

"Yes sir, it is. Samuel Rigdon. His brother and some others

are behind me in the barn covered with canvas." As he was
speaking, Captain Hauser was beginning to get a glimmer of
an idea. "They need buryin', Mister Jensen."

"Are you alone, Captain?"

"No. Miz Rigdon's at the house with Amilie an' two of my
men who got hurt durin' a gunfight yesterday."

Elder Jensen looked at his companions. Deacon Cobb was
blank-faced and perspiring. His wife was being brave with
great effort. Elder Jensen's wife, a tall, handsome woman
with startlingly large blue eyes, looked first at her husband
to see if he was going to speak, and when it seemed he was
not going to, she said, "I'd like to go to the house, Captain."

His hard-set features considered the blue-eyed woman for
a moment, then he inclined his head. "Miz Rigdon needs
someone, ma'am." As the tall woman started across the yard,
Hauser's pale gaze followed her. Instinct told him she would
be patient and tolerant up to a point. Beyond that point she
could probably make a man's hair stand straight up when
she got angry.

Elder Jensen led his horse toward the barn to care for it.
The Cobbs dutifully followed the elder's example, all of them
eyeing the large man with the carbine from time to time as
they entered the barn.

Captain Hauser studied them while pondering a scheme
he'd been considering since the four of them had stepped
off out front. When Elder Jensen returned from putting his
leggy speckled horse in a stall, Hauser gestured with his
carbine barrel. "Those are the men that need burying."

Jensen went over, looked beneath the canvas, let it drop,
and shook his head in the direction of the Cobbs. "It's them,
may God give peace to their souls." He removed his coat with
slow movements, folded it across a saddlepole, and waited
until Deacon Cobb had done the same, then he said, "Captain, you care to lend a hand? It's hot work buryin' folks this
time of year."

The deacon's wife edged toward the front opening. None

of the men paid any attention. Frank Hauser put aside the Winchester. He could hardly refuse to assist the diggers even though it would make him late catching up with his men and the wagons.

Jensen said, "How about the one on the porch?"

He got his answer while Hauser was rolling up sleeves that exposed arms like oak stumps. "Miz Rigdon showed me where she wants him buried. Out behind the house under an old tree." Hauser faced around. "He was her baby."

Elder Jensen watched Frank Hauser as he said, "Mind telling us what happened down here?"

Frank Hauser was looking around for digging tools. "No. There are others that can tell you. Right now I'll help you bury these fellers, but I can't spend the whole day here."

"Are your injured men bad off, Captain?"

"Bad enough. One is real bad off."

"Maybe I can help."

"You a doctor, Mister Jensen?"

"I'm experienced in the laying on of hands, Captain."

Hauser pointed. "Digging tools. Let's get this over with."

The shorter man said, "Someone's comin' from the house."

Hauser went to look out there, and nodded to himself. Hoskins should have remained in the house; at least it was cool in there. He called to him.

"We're goin' to dig graves."

Hoskins entered the barn, stared at the men standing deeper in the shadows, curtly nodded to them, and blew out a ragged breath. He'd dug graves. Every man has one particular thing he dislikes doing above everything else. Hoskins watched the others go after digging tools and swore under his breath. He could have left this country yesterday in good spirits. Now, when he finally was able to leave it, he wouldn't be in good spirits. Digging graves and putting people down into them upset him for days.

As Frank Hauser handed him a shovel, Hoskins said, "What about him on the porch?"

"Him too," the big man replied.

"Well, that's goin' to be bad, Cap. His mother should be there and—"

"Come along," the big man growled, and led the way out behind the barn. He spat on his hands, squinted at the location of the sun, and began pounding at the hard ground, first with a crowbar to get past the first eight inches of hardpan, then with his shovel. He scowled as he dug and sweated. He'd be lucky if he overtook the wagons and his men after midnight. More likely he wouldn't overtake them until tomorrow.

CHAPTER 22

Toward Sunset

THE grave diggers took in about as much water as they sweated out, but they never slackened and there was very little conversation as they worked.

Frank Hauser worked like a man with a job to do and the persistence to complete it no matter what, but Ace Hoskins's face got longer and longer as he sweated over an adjoining grave. The deacon and the elder worked methodically, doing something neither was a stranger to and doing it as men would who were prepared to accept the end of human lives any time of the day.

At the house, Amilie told Colby what the men were doing out behind the barn and asked whether or not he thought it would be wise to move Knight, whose bleeding had stopped but whose persisting lethargy had not changed since an hour or two after the shooting.

Colby felt better, still weak but with the advantage of having lost less blood than Henry Knight, and having been in excellent physical condition. He felt pretty good, except for the pain in his middle when he moved, so he thought he should be up and around, doing something regardless of what it was since everyone else was ambulatory and busy, including Elizabeth, who was staying occupied in her kitchen. The tall, blue-eyed woman and the deacon's wife kept busy setting the house to rights, putting rummaged drawers back where they belonged, peeking in at Knight from time to time, and for the most part saying very little.

When Amilie brought a meal of solid food to Colby, he ate

like a starving man and, under her watchful gaze, drank more water than she'd seen him drink before, even when they'd both come in from the worst of their horseback odyssey.

Only when he asked for his britches did she show her iron. She told him there was no need for him to leave the bed. She also told him the men behind the barn were about ready to lower the corpses and cover them, and that Captain Hauser was scrubbing out back as though he might finally be preparing to ride out.

She was right; Captain Hauser had left the final covering to Jensen and Cobb. His order to Ace Hoskins was to rig out the captain's horse and get something from Elizabeth to put in his saddlebags for the long ride southeastward.

Amilie was still with Colby when Hoskins appeared in the kitchen doorway where Elizabeth looked inquiringly at him. He mentioned a bundle of food for the captain and Elizabeth turned her back on him, which prevented Hoskins from seeing her face, but which also left him standing there unsure whether she'd understood him or not.

She had, but for a while she simply stood with her back to the doorway looking stonily at a blank wall; then she began making up the bundle and Hoskins meandered down the dingy hallway to look in on Knight.

When Hoskins left, Elizabeth wiped both hands on her apron and went out to the wash house where Frank Hauser was putting on his shirt after scrubbing. He smiled at her. She did not smile back. She said, "Please, Captain, not yet."

He nodded and ran bent fingers through his moist hair. "No, ma'am. Not yet." He stepped out and looked in the direction of the unkempt old cottonwood tree, said nothing until she came a little closer to speak again. "Not until he'll be in the shade."

"Yes'm." He turned slowly to face her. "When we leave, will you come with us?"

"No. I belong here."

He did not believe staying would be good for her. In fact, he knew it wouldn't, but he would be helpless against her determination and he knew that too. Still, he made the effort. "Down at Rosalia there's some decent folks, stores, more comforts and all."

She looked up at him, and smiled softly down around the mouth. She understood what he was trying to do, and warmed to him for it, but, as she told him again, the years of her life were here, all of them, since young girlhood. The bad ones, the springtime ones, and the sad ones. Even if she went with him down to Rosalia, the greatest part of her would never be unmindful of this place. As she said, "Forty years in one place marks a person forever. I'll never be able to turn the clock back and correct the mistakes, but away from here I'd never be able to belong elsewhere. Do you understand?"

He leaned very suddenly and kissed her cheek, then grabbed his hat and strode away in search of the diggers to bring them around to the cottonwood tree.

Elizabeth stood with a rough hand on her cheek, watching him cross out of sight in the direction of the barn. She went into tree-shade and sat down, eyes dry, mouth firm, conscious of the yearning of a heart starved too long for what Frank Hauser represented, which she had never got from Sidney and now would never get.

The elder and deacon dutifully and silently began digging in cottonwood shade. The elder's handsome, tall wife brought them water, watched the grave widen and deepen for a while, then returned to the house where Ace Hoskins was standing midway in the dingy hallway, leaning against a rough-board wall.

She paused, expecting him to speak, and when he didn't she went on out to the kitchen where the deacon's wife was helping Elizabeth make up the bundle of food for Frank Hauser. She asked if either of them had looked in on Henry Knight. Neither of them had.

She returned to the hallway and would have spoken, but

Hoskins's gaze was fixed unblinkingly and unseeingly ahead. She tiptoed past, entered the shadowy bedroom, and stood at the bedside.

Henry Knight was dead.

She felt for the chair, sank down, and turned, seeking a ray of slanting sunshine from the side wall. She did not move until someone shuffled to the doorway behind and said, "Is he dead?"

She looked around at Hoskins. "Didn't you know?"

"Yes'm. I guess I knew. I've known him a long time. We rode together on many trails. I'm goin' to miss him."

When the handsome, tall woman arose and turned, Hoskins was no longer in the doorway. Elizabeth's voice in the parlor brought the elder's wife out where Elizabeth and Captain Hauser were talking. On the porch, visible through the open door, were her husband and the deacon, backs to the blanketed corpse behind them.

Amilie came from Colby's room. Frank Hauser reached for Elizabeth's hand and squeezed it, then left the house as Elizabeth passed Amilie on her way to her own room.

The men lifted Samuel, blanket and all, went carefully down off the porch and around the house to cottonwood shade where there was a deep hole in the dark earth, and put Samuel down. There was no sign of Ace Hoskins, but when Amilie turned after she and the elder's wife had trooped out back with the men, Colby was holding to a rear doorjamb. Amilie let out a sharp breath that brought the elder's wife around to also stare.

Colby started toward them, fully dressed except for his shell-belt and gun. They got on each side of him.

Captain Hauser stood watching the back door. No one said a word; even the birds who lived in the top of the old tree were silent.

When Elizabeth appeared, her hair had been brushed and put up, she was attired in a powder-blue dress with white-lace cuffs. She was clutching a small handkerchief in one hand. Amilie had never seen that dress before, nor had she ever seen Elizabeth look the way she did now, not exactly serene but certainly not at all grim and suffering as she'd always looked as far back as Amilie could remember.

She had a small, dog-eared Bible which she handed to Frank Hauser. It had a scrap of paper midway through. She stood close to him.

The burial was accomplished quickly, solemnly, and efficiently. Deacon Cobb orated. Elder Jensen spoke briefly, and Frank Hauser opened the Bible to the place Elizabeth had marked and read two paragraphs, closed the book, and nodded his head.

Amilie would have taken Elizabeth inside, but she stood like stone as the men lowered Samuel and began covering him. She crumbled moist earth with one hand and with both eyes closed, breathed her own silent prayer, but she would not leave. Not even when it was finished, the grave had been properly mounded to allow for later settling, and Amilie had taken Colby back inside.

She was still out there motionless, silent and dry-eyed, when Captain Hauser appeared from the direction of the barn and said, "I'm obliged for the bundle."

She turned her face and slowly nodded.

"If you ever decide different," he told her, "I'll be down at Rosalia."

"If I ever do," she replied, "you'll be the person I'll look for. But I won't."

"I spoke to the elder and the deacon. They and their wives want you to accompany them up to St. George for a while. Until you want to come back. They'll look after you up there, Missus Rigdon."

Her lips quivered so she closed them hard. "For a short while?"

"Yes. For a short while."

"Do you think I should go with them, Captain?"

"You need it, for a while, for as long as you like, but you

need to leave this place at least until everything is manage-
able, Missus Rigdon."

She smiled softly at him. "You are married?"

"Yes'm."

"Your wife is a very fortunate woman, Captain. Good-bye.
I'll never forget you."

He held out a big hand, and she lay her fingers in it. Each
of them squeezed, then he turned and went around the side
of the house in the direction of the barn where solemn
people were putting the last blanket-shrouded body into the
back of an old wagon to which Hoskins had harnessed two
horses with collar-marks to indicate they were broke to drive.
Colby was down there sitting in shade under the watchful
eye of Amilie Prescott, who was trailing the reins of her big
colt and holding a lead-rope to Colby's mule-nosed bay
horse.

Captain Hauser eyed the preparations for departure with
an experienced eye before turning to pump the hands of the
elder and deacon as he said, "Take care of her, gents. She
never needed friends like she does now."

Amilie handed the reins to Colby and walked briskly
toward the rear of the house where Elizabeth was holding
her little handkerchief to her face. When the girl appeared,
Elizabeth turned her back for a moment. When she turned
around again she smiled.

Amilie could have counted the number of times Elizabeth
had smiled at her on the fingers of both hands. She smiled
back.

The two women came into each other's arms and remained
that way until Elizabeth had control again and pushed clear
with shiny eyes to say, "I know what you'd like to ask me, an'
I wish to God I could give you an answer, Amilie. Sidney
never mentioned it, so I don't know what happened out
there to your paw."

The girl accepted that. The lump in her throat was not for

a father she barely remembered anyway, it was for the tall, gaunt, strangely handsome woman in the powder-blue dress with little lace cuffs who had never before in all the years Amilie had known her looked handsome.

"Someday I'll come back and visit," the girl said. "I owe you."

"No you don't, dear. I wanted to be a mother to you, but it just wasn't in me. I'm sorry about that, Amilie. Someday I'd like to have you come visit."

This was very painful for them both, and Elizabeth had been just about drained dry of emotion over the past two days so she hugged the lithe girl again and turned her away as she said, "Don't keep the captain waiting. An' don't worry about me. Good-bye, Amilie."

After the girl was gone Elizabeth turned back toward the neatly mounded grave and raised the little balled-up hand-kerchief again. Furtive movement caught her attention be-yond tree-shade southward; she mopped her eyes and looked out there.

A fox was sitting in plain sight looking at her. It did not run when she lowered her hand with the handkerchief in it. It did not leave, in fact, until the sound of an old creaky wagon grinding out of the yard to the accompaniment of mounted men riding with it disrupted the deathly silence behind the house.

Then it did not flee, it turned westward and trotted away in its customary gait. Elizabeth, who had seen dozens of foxes, watched it with a sense of something eerie. Eventually she returned to the house, passed through to the porch, and stood in shade looking out where the wagon and its mounted travelers were beginning to angle more southward than eastward.

From down in front of the barn, the elder's wife saw Elizabeth up there and crossed slowly to join her.

The day was well spent; it would be too late to leave now.

Besides, her husband and the deacon would be starved. Digging graves was exhausting work.

The sun was well off-center by the time the dust faded and the land looked empty again.

CHAPTER 23

The Night Birds

IT was a long ride, not because the wagons had made good progress but because when Captain Hauser had left them to reach the Rigdon place he'd had to cover a lot of miles, and these had to now be covered again, as well as the additional miles the wagon cavalcade had traveled.

It was open country where the roadway divided the land. Visibility was good in all directions, which had been especially gratifying for the Rangers. They had seen skulkers on their back-trail, not well organized, more often than not one or two horsemen by themselves, at the most four or five where they would come together and sit watching the distant cavalcade, but there were rocks along the way, occasionally in massive disarray, large and deep enough to conceal ambushers, and that worried the Rangers. Their first night out they'd made a fireless camp and kept a sharp watch through the dark hours.

There had been no attack, but by morning light they found sign of skulkers who had tried to sneak up where the horses had been herded under guard.

They might have been set afoot despite the guards except for one of Captain Hauser's innovations. He'd lost a number of horses to night-stalkers in his time. His response had been steel-chain hobbles. Without a key to the locks, thieves could not stampede the animals. The captain had first seen such hobbles used in Texas, where ingenious horse thieves had developed countermeasures to just about every other method employed to thwart them. They never devised a way to remove steel-chain hobbles, which was fortunate for the company of Rangers, whose slow progress out of the Wolf Hole country could not be improved upon as long as they were burdened by the laden wagons, and they would not have abandoned the wagons under any circumstances. Those heavy little printing presses were the best evidence obtainable, along with the crates of uncirculated, newly printed counterfeit greenbacks, anyone could present in a court of law.

By mid-afternoon Captain Hauser began to worry. There was no sighting of the wagons. He sent Ace Hoskins loping ahead to scout.

Hoskins returned ahead of a blood-red sunset to report that the Ranger complement was about four miles southward and still moving.

The captain changed course slightly to make an interception down where he thought the cavalcade would probably fort up for the night.

He hadn't said much since leaving the Rigdon place. He had smoked one of his cherished cheroots and had seemed lost in a solemn reverie most of the time. Once, he dropped back beside the old wagon and asked Colby how he was faring.

Except for a swollen, discolored, and sore middle, Colby was doing well enough. Amilie rode beside the wagon to keep an eye on him.

Hoskins drifted back after returning from his scout to tell Colby what he knew about the company, and before riding ahead looked solemnly at the blanket-shrouded body of his old friend.

The original idea had been for Colby to ride flat on his back in the wagon, but he'd ended up tooling the team, which meant he sat up there where the springs beneath the seat cushioned him from most of the bumps. But sitting was more uncomfortable than lying flat. Since there was no one else to drive the wagon, he did it and smiled at Amilie even when he did not feel much like smiling. The wound that had torn flesh on his side and arm prevented him from handling the lines with both hands, but since the horses Hoskins had gotten back at the ranch were steady plodders, he didn't need both hands.

With the sun sinking lower, Captain Hauser called back to Amilie asking about water up ahead where they could set up camp for the night.

She told him that there was no water for at least five miles, so Hauser continued to ride, and Amilie looked exasperatedly at his broad back as she spoke aside to Colby. "Typical. When a man needs something from a woman he talks to her, otherwise she might as well be a stone."

Colby eyed her pensively. "Some men maybe."

She turned. "Yes, some men."

He laughed.

Visibility began to lessen as the late day wore along. Once, Captain Hauser halted, watching a solitary horseman on their left a fair distance. It was impossible to make out much except that whoever he was he'd seen them and was watching as they moved slowly across the land.

He made no move to approach and neither did he turn back southward. The captain gestured for the wagon to strike out again, and for as long as they could see that distant, motionless figure they watched it, but as visibility became more limited it was more difficult to see him. In the end they did not quite ignore the strange horseman, but they were not greatly concerned about him either.

Colby sent Amilie up ahead to lead the way after dusk arrived. Captain Hauser accepted this situation without comment. She took them closer to the road and, like a homing pigeon, unerringly to a large field of scattered gray boulders where several trees grew and there was a spring-fed pool of very blue water.

It wasn't much of a camp. There was plenty of food from Elizabeth's bundle, at least for this meal and breakfast, and there was horse-feed among the rocks. The camp was less than a hundred yards from the roadway.

They sat together without a fire, finished their meal, and carried on a desultory conversation after the fashion of tired men. They also avoided all mention of what lay behind them until Amilie spoke up, unable to see the expression of disapproval on the faces of the men.

She said, "Elizabeth wasn't convinced there was a cache until I showed her the money and told her what it was. She said even when she told me about it she wasn't plumb sure it existed. She said her husband made real free with the truth."

The men remained silent until Hoskins dryly commented. "Someone sure believed it existed, otherwise them fellers wouldn't have come lookin' for it when anyone with a lick of sense wouldn't have gone near that yard."

Amilie did not dispute this, but she said, "You're talkin' about Joseph. Well, he wasn't real sure either, was he?"

Hoskins looked owlishly at the girl. "Why wasn't he?"

"If he'd known about it for sure, would they have ran-sacked the house and torn everything up looking for more when they already had the money?"

Although that was not flawless logic, no one chose to argue with the girl. To get off a subject which was too near and too unpleasant, Colby said, "I'd bet money that was an Indian watching us."

This possibility had evidently occurred to the other men. Captain Hauser said, "Likely. Navajos aren't real trouble-some by nature. All the same, it wouldn't hurt to sleep with an eye open tonight."

He'd barely said that when a night bird called from across the road somewhere, which would not have caused hair to stand up on the men's necks if another night bird hadn't answered from the opposite direction.

Frank Hauser pulled his carbine from its boot among the tangle of saddlery and harness and looked around for rocks large enough to conceal his frame. Colby and Ace Hoskins also got their weapons and moved back and apart from each other seeking shelter.

Where Amilie went, without being aware of it for a few minutes, was among the same boulders that were shielding Frank Hauser. She made this discovery when she reached to smooth the ground before sitting down, and a gunbarrel appeared between two gray rocks. She waited for the weapon to be cocked. Nothing happened. She was almost holding her breath when a man's exasperated soft curse sounded from among the boulders behind her and Captain Hauser appeared, crouching as he came forward.

He had wedged the carbine in place to hold her attention while he flanked her. It might not have worked every time, but it certainly worked this time, except that when the lithe girl discovered how she had been duped, she sprang up mad enough to chew nails and spit rust.

Captain Hauser held up a huge hand. "Quiet! Choke to death if you want to, but don't make any noise!"

She was rigid in her anger. It wasn't just being made a fool of that made her furious, it was an accumulation of exasperating paradoxes about the big man that had alternately softened her toward him and made her furious with him.

He came closer, holstered his Colt, reached to lift the carbine from between the rocks, then did it to her again. He handed her the carbine as he quietly said, "You'd ought to have something to protect yourself with, girl."

Then he turned his back to her and sat on the ground where he could see beyond their place of concealment, as though he didn't care whether she stood like that all night or relaxed.

She could not sustain her fury indefinitely. After a while she sank to one knee, leaning on the Winchester, also looking past into the moonless night.

The next time a night bird called it was closer; she guessed it was either in the road or on their side of it. She waited a long time before the other night bird answered, and this time she did not remember she was furious with the bear of a man beside her.

"I'm scairt."

Captain Hauser's answer was matter-of-factly given. "That's a healthy reaction."

The night was utterly still. Normally it would have been possible to hear the horses cropping grass or browse. Even the horses were silent.

She whispered to him. "Indians?"

He replied in the same matter-of-fact tone of voice. "Maybe. But if they're after horses they're in for a surprise."

"Can you see where Ashe and Mister Hoskins went?"

"No," he replied, and took time off from his searching vigil to look at her profile. "You still got that little gun you shot that feller with back in the yard?"

"Yes, inside my shirt. Why? Do you want it?"

"No. I just wondered is all, because years back on two occasions when there was trouble, women with guns were behind me, an' both times they got to shootin' wild. Neither of 'em hit me but I swore then I'd never let another armed female get behind me if there was trouble."

She looked at him. "I'm not behind you."

"No, an' you're not goin' to get behind me."

A night bird called and this time there was no answer. Amilie whispered something that was more a hope than a fact. "They're not supposed to attack in the dark."

Captain Hauser's reply to that was as dry as old corn husks. "I've seen a lot of graves of folks who believed that, young lady."

Neither of them spoke again for a long while, not until a man's voice bellowed in the darkness. It was not the voice of either Colby or Ace Hoskins. If the big man hadn't been beside her, Amilie would have believed he could have been responsible. It was a deep, resonant voice, the kind that would belong to a large man.

"You fellers with the wagon? Who are you an' what're you doin' out here?"

Captain Hauser swore, moments before Ace Hoskins sang out in unmistakable relief. "Clancy! You like to scairt the whey out of me."

The booming voice answered immediately. "That you, Ace?"

"Yeah. Me'n Ashe Colby an' Cap Hauser."

The booming voice returned. "Well, we got to worrying so a couple of us come back to see if we was bein' follered."

Hauser struggled to his feet to begin climbing out of his hiding place. He asked the man with the loud voice who was with him. The answer came from an altogether different direction. "Joe Silver."

"Come over to the wagon," Hauser said, and looked back to offer Amilie a hand. It was tricky, scrambling among rocks in the dark, and someone with a broken ankle would be another damned burden.

She accepted the extended hand to balance her way clear, then Captain Hauser pulled his hand free, turned his back on her, and went off in the direction of the old wagon where two men were leaning over the sideboards looking at something wrapped in an old blanket. He came up behind them, and neither man turned even when he spoke to them.

Colby and Hoskins materialized out of the darkness on the opposite side of the wagon.

The man with the booming voice was as tall as Frank Hauser, but rangy, rawboned, and younger. His companion was compact, shorter, and with the dark eyes and complexion of a Mexican, which in fact he was not.

Amilie did not appear until they had spoken quietly about Henry Knight in his shroud, and this set the mood for all of them when she came to hand back the captain's saddlegun. Both newcomers glanced at her, then glanced away, until the dark-eyed man named Silver turned very slowly back and looked again.

Colby introduced her. Clancy, who hadn't bothered to look very close, showed more astonishment at her plainness than Joe Silver did, but neither of them commented.

Captain Hauser wanted to know how far ahead the wagons were with the rest of the company. Clancy airily gestured. "Maybe four, five miles down the road." He dropped his arm to ask a question. "You see any riders skulkin' along back yonder?"

"One rider south of us. He sat watching us go by until it got too dark to see him. Most likely a reservation Indian. But no one north up your back-trail."

"Well, there's been a few now an' then," stated Clancy, rolling his glance around to Amilie again. Sure as hell she was a female but . . .

"Everything all right down yonder where you're camped?" the captain asked, drawing the rawboned, big man's attention away from the girl. "Yeah. But that feller named Hanson died this afternoon. Wasn't much hope for him from the start. Otherwise, we got complained at a lot by the prisoners but that's about all, except for an old scrawny weasel named Rigdon tryin' for all he's worth to bribe us to turn him loose. Claimed he had a cache of sound money, an' if we'd just go back where he's got it hid . . ." Clancy ruefully wagged his head.

No one told him old Rigdon had been telling the truth.

The men went to the eating site and dropped tiredly down. Amilie listened to their conversation from beneath the old wagon where she only began to feel the chill along toward midnight or slightly after. Colby came over and tossed a smelly saddle blanket to her as he leaned down to say, "Good night. I'll get you another blanket if you want it."

She wanted it, but instead of asking she said, "Get one for yourself. You've been overdoing it all day. You don't want to collapse tomorrow, do you? Then you better bed down and get some sleep."

He walked away, returned in fifteen minutes while the

conversation among the other men was still going on, crawled beneath the old wagon with another saddle blanket, and made himself comfortable. Amilie watched everything he did until he turned his head and smiled. Then she said, "There's a lot of country out there, this isn't the only place for you to bed down. Besides, they're goin' to notice."

"Let 'em," he told her. "Amilie?"

"What."

"Well, you've been real helpful."

She watched his face in the semidarkness beneath the old wagon. "So have you, Ashe."

". . . Do you know how old I am?"

"You said something about that once before. No, I don't know how old you are."

"Thirty-five."

"I guess a lot of folks are, aren't they?"

"You're goin' on nineteen. I'm sixteen years older'n you are."

"I'm not real good at ciphering; is that how it figures out?"

"Sixteen years. That's darned near old enough to be your paw."

She got a vertical line in the middle of her forehead between the eyes. "Do you want me to feel sorry for you because you're old? Hell, Ashe, look how old Sidney was an' he could still rope better'n either of his boys."

He turned facing towards the slats of the wagonbed and was quiet for a long time, until she leaned to see him better and said, "Is today your birthday? Is that why you brought up bein' thirty-five years old?"

He did not look at her. "Go to sleep, Amilie."

"No. Not yet." She was still wearing a puzzled frown as she leaned looking down at him. "Ashe?"

"What."

". . . Do you like me, is that what this is all about?"

He met her gaze. "I like you, Amilie."

"Well, hell, why'd you talk about bein' old an' all?"

"So's you'd know I'm too old for you."

She continued to stare at him. "You're not too old for me. I'm a woman—well—I know what folks think when they look at me. But no matter how folks always think I'm real young, I'm not. An' you want to know somethin' else?" She did not even allow him time enough to draw a breath, let alone form words. "I never liked men. None of 'em. You don't have to know a hundred of 'em not to like 'em. But I liked you right from the start. Otherwise I wouldn't have given you my most precious treasure, my paw's little gambler's gun. . . . Would I have?"

When she stopped speaking Colby became suddenly acutely conscious of the silence over where the men were sitting. He looked out there. They weren't even moving. It was as though something had turned them all to statues.

Every word Amilie had said had carried that far, and farther. On a dead-silent night like this one, even a whisper carried.

He turned back, placed a hand across her lower face, drew her down to him under the old saddle blankets with their aroma of drying sweat, and held her close. When he removed the hand, she snuggled against him with her head on his shoulder like a puppy.

CHAPTER 24

A Riddle of Foxes

THEY didn't catch up to the Ranger company until shortly before noon, and they'd struck camp before sunup. On horseback they'd have covered the distance in half that time.

Joe Silver rode ahead to stop the captured wagons; otherwise it might have taken even longer for Hauser's little group to catch up.

Where they met was near some cottonwood trees. Once, there had been a one-roomed sod house near those trees, where some bold—and foolish—soul had set up housekeeping back before it was safe to do anything like that. The walls still stood, as no doubt their builder had known they would, but the roof had fallen in after having fire-arrows shot into it.

Amilie watched Colby, Hoskins, and Frank Hauser go among the noisy men calling back and forth. There was less exuberation when the Rangers saw the shroud in the Rigdon wagon, and after that, even when they built a fire to make coffee by, the exuberance was leavened. The men had all known Frank Knight.

Colby brought her a tin plate of stew with coffee and sat apart with her while the sun climbed. He pointed out some of the strangers and told her anecdotes about them. There was, for instance, a beefy, unwashed, dark man they called Paco. Colby did not tell her the rest of his name, but he told her that Paco was part Mexican and part Apache, and although he was forever smiling and joking, he could track a fly across a piece of glass and kill a man at thirty feet with a knife.

The company had their prisoners chained in the first wagon. Amilie strolled down there when Colby went back to help water the horses over where the gutted jacal stood. Sidney Rigdon's eyes popped wide at sight of her. He recovered very quickly and called her close as he said, "Was they at the ranch?"

She nodded.

"Well, girl, out with it."

"Your wife went north with some people from St. George. She took your cache with her."

Sidney's brows furrowed. "She done what?"

Amilie ignored the questions. "There was a fight in the yard. Some men got shot."

"Who got shot, Amilie?"

"Joseph and Sam'l. They got killed, some others got hurt too. They got buried out back of the barn, except for Sam'l, your wife wanted him planted under that old tree behind the house."

Rigdon eased back, rattling his chains as he did so. The other prisoners looked solemnly at Amilie. They had heard, and none of what she'd said had improved their morale. But old Rigdon had his gaze fixed miles away to the northwest. He might as well have been somewhere else, alone and unfettered, for all the attention he paid to what was going on around him.

The Rangers treated their prisoners fairly but roughly. After feeding them they made sure the chains were still in place, and with Frank Hauser out front, the company with its three wagons started southward again, and this time there was no halt until a scout returned from farther along to report that there was an uninhabited rancheria about two miles ahead, with springwater.

They left the road, reached the empty hogans, made camp, and while the others were caring for the livestock,

Colby took Amilie over to one of the hogans and looked inside. Usually these inverted beehive residences that had been unoccupied since the previous summer had spiders galore and a number of other inhabitants. This one not only had no wildlife, it smelled of cooking.

Colby left Amilie over there, went in search of grinning Paco, and told him what they'd found. Paco rolled his one good eye—the other one sometimes rolled of its own accord but not this time—and said, "They knew we was comin' an went away." He waved with a thick arm. "Out there somewhere. They been here, not long, maybe couple of weeks, but they been gettin' settled in again. Mostly, the clans already are at their special places. This bunch was late gettin' up here." Paco smiled broadly. "They're out there watchin'. They're fox-people. I seen their signs. They'll come back after we're gone." Paco's smile hardened into a fixed death's-head expression without much humor. "They're scairt of us, an' they got reason to be. You want to bed down in the hogan, go ahead."

Before Colby got back to the hogan, Captain Hauser intercepted him. "Lots of times when someone's on a trail they bring back a horse, or maybe some guns. . . . What are you goin' to do with the girl? She can't hang around the barracks, Ashe."

Although none of this was said antagonistically, it annoyed Colby. "I'll find a place for her. There's jobs in Rosalia."

The big man stood gazing steadily at Colby. "That don't cover all of it," he said quietly. "You understand what I mean?"

Colby understood, but had difficulty answering. "She couldn't have stayed back yonder. Not after her helpin' me an' all."

The big man stood like a rock, saying nothing and waiting.

"Well, I'm not exactly sure, Cap. She an' I'll work somethin' out."

Hauser barely inclined his head. "You do that, Ashe, an' you remember—you don't keep her as a pet."

Colby was red in the face as the big man turned away in response to someone's yell. When he returned to the hogan, Amilie was inside with two candles lighted and a cooking-fire burning in the stone ring directly below the smoke-hole. She smiled inquiringly as he sat down, considered the hot meal she'd prepared, and said, "The Indians who own this place left when they saw us coming. Paco says they'll come back after we leave. Amilie?"

"Yes."

". . . What is that stuff you're cooking?"

She wasn't sure. "Meat rolled in coarse flour, an' a tin of vegetables. They didn't have any coffee."

"What kind of meat, Amilie?"

"It's not mutton, Ashe. Mutton's got a different smell. I'm not sure what it is. Maybe deer meat." She held up a sliver hot from the pan for him to taste. He took it gingerly, examined it by firelight, then popped it into his mouth. "You're right. It's deer meat."

He was wrong. It was dog meat.

She filled two tin plates and handed him one. They ate mostly in silence. Outside, there was a large cooking fire and considerable activity. There were guards out in all directions, and the prisoners had been pulled from the wagon, chains in place, pushed down at the fire and fed. Eventually, they were included in the desultory supperfire conversation.

Sidney Rigdon was raffish and sly as always. Shock over the death of his two sons had evidently not lasted very long. Another of the prisoners, a man with hair to his shoulders and a trimmed auburn beard, coarse, rugged features and the eyes of a fanatic, argued at length about the legitimacy of counterfeiting by people whose history included discrimination and hostility all the way from upstate New York to the Promised Land west of the Missouri. He exclaimed that "Gentiles" would not hire his people, would not even trade with them if there was an alternative, and began reciting a litany of wrongs perpetrated against his people that was cut short by a hard-eyed man with a livid knife scar on one cheek who had been smoking a pipe and who removed it to interrupt the speaker in a voice as quietly menacing as a sheathed knife.

"Tell us about the Mountain Meadows Massacre, brother. Tell us about the Brotherhood of Assassins, the Danites. Tell us about holy murder an' nightriders."

The fanatic eyed the man with the scarred face. He probably would have replied, but Frank Hauser stopped the discussion by saying, "We'll make Rosalia by tomorrow night if we get an early enough start. If not, we'll get there day after tomorrow. Until then, there won't be any more talk about who you are or who we are. Now, let's douse the fire, set guards, an' bed down."

The captain's word was law. Colby saw the fire dying through the doorless opening of the hogan and went outside for a while. He met Ace Hoskins leading a pair of team horses out to be hobbled. Hoskins nodded to him without stopping.

He strolled down closer to the wagons and encountered several men he had ridden out with. One of them asked if what he'd heard about the girl shooting someone at a ranch back up yonder was true. Colby said it was and the Ranger wagged his head. "You better not roil her, partner."

Colby smiled because he was supposed to and because the other man had smiled when he'd said that, but the impression Colby took back to the hogan with him was that, because of Amilie, when the other men thought of him, they did so in a frame of mind that included the girl, and that would eventually set him apart from the rest of them.

He said nothing about this as he dropped down by the fire with her across from him. Partly because he did not want to add to her problems and partly because she had scrubbed until her face shone by soft firelight, and had managed somehow to comb and brush her hair. She looked more female this night than she'd ever looked before to him, bruises and all.

She pointed where two blankets had been laid out as bedding. They were a respectable distance apart. "They're oleots," she told him, and when that drew a blank look, she explained. "Sometimes The People make blankets of the wool of sheep no more'n six months old. It's not as tough as their regular blankets, but it's as soft as cotton an' a hell of a lot nicer an' warmer."

He looked around. "Where did you find them?"

She pointed toward what appeared to be a mound of old rags. "Under there . . . Ashe?"

"Yes."

"We'd ought to leave some money behind for eatin' their food."

He was agreeable, then he smiled at her. "Not homemade money."

She did not smile back. She was regarding him steadily from across the little fire. "I want to ask you a question, but I don't want you to laugh at me."

"I won't laugh."

"Well, when I was sitting out there with the horses when we first came near the yard an' you was in the barn, a red fox trotted in front of me, stopped and looked at me, then trotted away."

He sat in silence watching her, thinking that she was very pretty.

"An' back at the house, I was lookin' out back where Elizabeth was sittin' near Sam'l's grave, and a red fox did the same thing to her: trotted along an' stopped to look at her, then trotted away. . . . That Mexican or whatever he is, the one named Paco, he said the Indians who live here belong to the fox clan. Do you get an odd feeling about—these things?"

He didn't. "No. There are lots of little foxes in country like this."

"I know that, but I've never seen 'em just trot up and stare at folks before. Every other time I've seen 'em, they ran off scairt as hell. . . . What is the fox clan?"

"Darned if I know, except that Indians'll adopt some animal as the totem of their clan, or their fightin' society or somethin' like that." He suddenly stopped speaking, sat up straight, and stared at her. "Just a minute. When I first struck out to go up north, I found a little she-fox with cubs. She had an infected foot an' her pups looked starved because she couldn't hunt. I roped her, pulled a thorn out of her foot, cleaned it up, and set her loose." He stared at her across the fire for a moment, then wagged his head. "Naw, those foxes you'n Elizabeth saw weren't tryin' to tell you anythin' or tryin' to reassure you everything would turn out all right. They can't talk to each other. The ones you saw couldn't know about me helpin' that other one."

"Then what were they doing?"

"I don't know."

"But I've seen dozens of them an' not once did any of them do anythin' but run like hell from me. Ashe, maybe that one you helped . . ."

"Amilie, that don't make a lick of sense."

From the doorway a man called softly. It was Ace Hoskins to ask if they needed any blankets or coffee in there. When Colby called back they had plenty of both, Hoskins said, "Then you got the only hogan they didn't take everything away from when they left. See you come sunup."

When Colby turned back, gazing at the very special, very soft oleots, at the little pile of rare firewood Amilie had used to make their supper, and at the food they'd left traces of in the tin plate, and finally raised his eyes to her face, she was regarding him with perfectly round eyes.

He used his good arm to fling his hat aside as he said, "Amilie, it just happened that way."

"How many hogans are around here, Ashe?"

"Well, about six."

"An' they're all stripped but the one we chose. Isn't that stretchin' coincidence a hell of a length?"

He frowned at her. "You're superstitious."

She smiled back. "I don't think so, but I sure as hell don't believe just critters with two legs have any corner on what happens in this life."

He stretched out with his head propped on one hand, looking at her. He was tired of the subject of mystical or spiritual foxes and was thinking of something else. "Amilie, when we get down to Rosalia we got to find a place for you to live. Maybe find you work around the town or maybe out at one of the ranches. An' I think you'd ought to stop swearing. I don't mind it. Well, at least I'm used to you doin' it, but women aren't supposed to cuss. If you do it around Rosalia, folks are goin' to leave you pretty much alone. Now don't get your back up. I'm just tryin' to explain somethin' to you."

She didn't get her back up. She sat across from him, listening and watching him. When he'd finished speaking, she said, "Ashe, how much do you like me?"

He had no more expected that than he expected the hogan's roof to fall in on them. "You know I like you, Amilie. I've told you that."

"But how much?"

"Well," he mumbled, and sat up again. "Considerable. After all, if it hadn't been for you back up yonder—"

"Oh dammit, forget that," she exclaimed. "That's behind us. Anyway, I needed you more'n you needed me. . . . How much?"

He looked around, saw his hat over by one of the oleots, and looked back. "Amilie, let me explain something to you. I already told you how old I am an'—"

"How damned much!"

"Don't cuss. It's not ladylike!"

"How much do you like me!"

He raised his eyes to her face. "More than any woman I've known."

She did not relent. "You ever been in love?"

He let his breath out slowly, still looking straight at her. "Yes, an' it's bothered me because you're so much younger—"

"I'm not that much younger; besides, Elizabeth told me one time that women are born old about some things. About bein' in love an' all."

"Amilie, you're not in love."

"I most certainly am an' I have been since about the time I gave you my little gun."

They stared at each other. Colby looked for his hat again, drew forth an old bandana, and mopped at his throat with it. Didn't seem likely a little dying fire could make the hogan as hot as it was.

He feebly smiled at her. "Dawn's goin' to come awful early, an' Cap has fits if everyone isn't ready to roll when he is."

"Ashe, will you marry me?"

He stopped mopping, very slowly got a pained expression on his face as he said, "How about those sixteen years, Amilie? Someday I'll be old an' you'll still—"

"If you ever bring that up again I'm goin' to wait until we're in a roomful of your friends with their wives and cuss a blue streak. . . . Ashe, just say yes or no."

He was stuffing the bandana away when it occurred to him he was the one who was supposed to ask that question, not her. But he had no intention of causing another outburst, so he nodded his head. "Yes'm. Will you marry me?"

She came up off the ground like a puma, stepped over the crimson coals, and almost bowled him over. "I'd have married you ten days ago," she said as her good arm curled impulsively around his neck.

He had to brace against her weight. "But you hate men."

Her eyes were moist in the diminishing light. "I do. I hate *men*—but not one *man*. Do they have a preacher in Rosalia?"

"Yes. Scrawny little cuss with a forked beard an' ears too big for his head."

"Will he marry us?"

"Yes. I don't know any reason why not."

". . . Do you love me, Ashe?"

"I love you, Amilie. I've loved you for some time now."

That one arm was very strong. "An' I love you and I never thought I'd be able to say that to a man."

He looked over where his hat was near one of the oleots. He kissed her twice, then went over where his hat was lying.